WOLFBRAT

WOLFBANE SERIES: BOOK 3.5

CELIA HART

Celia Hart LLC

Content Warning

These content notes are made available here so readers can inform themselves, if they want to. Some readers might consider these "spoilers." If you don't like spoilers, look away. You've been warned.

- **Bad language**: strong and frequent

- **Sex**: some descriptions of sexual acts

- **Violence**: some descriptions of violent acts

- **Other**: bullying, homophobia, misogyny, pregnancy, purity culture, sexual harassment, slut-shaming

If you'd like more information on any of the above content notes prior to reading, please reach out (celia.hart.author@gmail.com) and I will be happy to elaborate so that you may make a fully informed decision before choosing to turn the page!

For anyone who ever felt misunderstood. We are all a bit of a brat inside.

Chapter 1

Rock bottom. That was where I found myself in late fall, with Libby flailing on the floor, her arms and legs banging against the worn linoleum of my parents' kitchen, her face wet, swollen, and red, screaming as if I were clawing her simply because I told her she had to take another bite of her lunch.

Libby was clearly getting a head start on the terrible twos.

I sighed and threw my head against the kitchen table. When Luke and I had finally marked each other, after years of being in love, I never envisioned I would end up here—a jobless single mom, living with my parents, and outcast of the pack. But here I was.

Libby's wails echoed throughout the small kitchen. My youngest brother, Neil, crept in, grabbing a can of soda from the fridge and giving his head a shake as he took in the scene. He had finally graduated from high school and turned eighteen earlier this year and was now the final member of the family to be recruited as a warrior, joining my dad, Jack, Kyle, and Mark. He already looked every bit the part, tall and muscled like the rest of the family. I couldn't believe that he had once been my baby brother.

"Thank Artemis I don't have a mate. Last thing I need is a *Libby*." He scrunched his nose at my daughter.

"Move the fuck out then!" I retorted. "Libby doesn't need you either!"

"Have you seen what junior warriors get paid?" He huffed.

"It was your choice to be one."

"I'm serving my pack. What the hell are you doing besides disturbing our peace with your little hellion? When are you finally going back to the packhouse?"

"Dude, just move out if you don't like it! Libby has as much right to disturb the peace with her crying as you do with the loud-as-fuck video games you and Mark play all the time! And let's not talk about the piss you leave all over the toilet seat. Can't you learn how to aim? And, oh, don't think Mom doesn't notice all your crusty washcloths when she does your laundry."

His cheeks reddened. Got him with that one. He turned without saying another word. *Ten bucks says he's going to start doing his own laundry now.*

Libby's howling finally turned to sniffs and hiccups. I breathed out a sigh of relief. I was tired, constantly exhausted. No matter what I did, I could never shake the low energy that had taken hold of me.

"Lucy!" my mom called out as she entered the kitchen. "Do you mind making your chocolate cake for tonight? Jack will be coming by with Tyler to share some news with the family, and I have a feeling we'll need to pull out a cake to celebrate." She smiled and winked as if she already knew what it was.

"Choco cake!" Libby brightened, standing up. At least she wasn't crying anymore.

"Yeah, sure," I replied, hoisting myself up out of my chair.

"I'm running to the grocery store now, so text me if you're missing any ingredients while I'm out," my mom said, walked over to Libby, and planted some kisses on her head. "Libby, be good for your mama, okay?"

"Mama!" Libby repeated. In my mind, I knew she meant, *Like hell I'm going to be good for my mama*!

But still, I forced myself to get to work, pulling out bowls, measuring cups, and my favorite raspberry-colored KitchenAid mixer that Luke had given me as a Christmas gift when I first moved into the packhouse. I quickly inventoried what we had and shot my mom a text of anything that was running low.

I handed a pan and wooden spoon to Libby to keep her entertained. After months of using this as an easy distraction, I'd gotten used to the banging—the soundtrack to my life. Bang, bang, bang. *Lucy, you made the wrong choice.* Bang, bang, bang. *That's what Luke's probably doing, but not with you.* Bang, bang, bang.

That evening, my brother Jack and his mate Tyler entered the house, engulfing everyone in hugs. "How's it going, Luce?" Jack asked, giving my shoulder a squeeze and narrowing his eyes in a sympathetic way, the light of the entryway reflecting off his blond lashes. What a sin that one of the males of the family got the perfect lashes when they would have been much better suited for me.

"Things are fine," I replied. I'd never really been close to any of my brothers. They just really didn't get me. They were always into teasing and wrestling each other, and playing sports in the backyard, while I played with my dolls by myself. Sometimes I convinced Kyle and Mark to play house with me, but it had never been often when the boys all had each other.

"Seriously, Luce, if there's anything you need, Tyler and I are both here for you."

"Thanks, appreciate it," I replied, "but I'm fine, honestly!" I tried my best to look the part. The last thing I needed was Jack telling Luke that I totally was not fine. No, I wanted him to believe I didn't need him and his impotent, cowardly ass. I was fucking hot and had once been recruited to be a supermodel. Men didn't break my heart. I broke theirs!

Okay, so Luke was the only man I'd ever kissed, dated, loved. And he was also the man who shattered my heart into a million pieces, more than once. But from here on out, no man would ever do that to me again, especially not Luke!

Sure, we had marked each other, and there was a nagging feeling that I was missing a piece of me. Sometimes the mark he'd given me itched, becoming inflamed with irritation. But I was strong. My whole family was warriors. And maybe I was useless out in the field, but I was not useless in life.

And then something else nagged at me—a voice I tried my best to ignore. *Ultimately, I was at least partially responsible for driving him away.*

A sharp pain reverberated within my chest. It was an icky feeling that I did my best to avoid.

"So, how's the OnlyFans going?" Tyler winked, pulling me in for a hug.

"Hardy har ha." The only reason I let him get away with it was because he was Tyler, and inappropriate jokes were basically his trademark.

"Don't worry, after Jack talked to him, Blake made it clear to the pack that if anyone else shares those pics they'll be in big trouble."

"What's he going to do? Stab them?"

Tyler chuckled. "I wouldn't put it past him. Pretty sure he's got a knife in every drawer of the packhouse. He once whipped one out of the diaper table in Ryker's room. Think he considered stabbing his own son for leaking baby poo all over him."

I couldn't help but let out a laugh. "Blake's crazy, but he's not that crazy."

"I think he's starting alpha training early. Desensitization to lethal weapons. Ryker's going to be more sadistic than he is."

I let out another chuckle.

"Cheer up, Lucy." He gave me a soft punch to the arm. "It could be worse. You could be chained up and getting stabbed in Blake's torture chamber. See? Not so bad anymore, right?" He paused for a moment, then added, "Though, the right kind of stabbing wouldn't be so bad." The sides of his mouth lifted in a mischievous grin.

"Who says I need to cheer up?" I narrowed my eyes at him.

"Well, I don't see you leaving your house, going to work, doing your biweekly sparring, or taking Libby out anywhere. So clearly something's not right." Had he told Luke all that? Did Luke notice that too? I straightened my shoulders, resolving that I'd finally take my ass back to work and sign up for a sparring session. Small steps.

Once Kyle and Emma arrived with their two pups, Ethan and Miles, we all took seats at the dining table, nine chairs squeezed around it, with me holding Libby on my lap, and Emma and Kyle holding their pups on theirs, both of whom coincidentally had been born on the same day in April, just one year apart. I think we were all anticipating an announcement of a third, since they all seemed to happen around this time of year. Neither of them was shy about how often they went at it. I wouldn't have normally minded, except nothing grossed me out more than knowing what one of my closest friends did with my brother!

Dinner went about as it normally did, with my brothers getting into belching contests, Kyle, Tyler, and Jack all bouncing jokes off each other, and my mom scurrying around the table making sure everyone had everything they needed, babying her mate and all of her sons.

Finally, my dad raised his voice. "Everyone!" We all turned toward him. "Jack has some news to share with us." He smiled widely, giving his son a squeeze on the shoulder, pride in his eyes.

"Don't worry, he didn't knock me up yet!" Tyler blurted out. "We're still open for babysitting."

Everyone chuckled.

Jack shook his head at Tyler with a smile on his face, then turned back to the table. "I wanted to make sure I let the family know before Blake announces it Sunday at temple. With Blake and Jasmine now having the added responsibility of parenthood and being overwhelmed with the work required to run a pack, they've decided to expand the leadership team." Jack paused for a moment, then continued, "Blake is adding a gamma to the team, and he asked me to take on the role."

"So proud of you, cuddle bear." Tyler pulled him in for a kiss. For a long time, Jack had shied away from these public displays of affection when Tyler would try to encourage them. He'd finally begun to accept them in the past few months, at least around our family.

My mom got up and ran over, wrapping her arms around Jack, swaying back and forth with his body in a tight grip. "My little pup is so grown up now. I'm so proud of you, Jacky."

"So, when's the ceremony?" Kyle asked.

"In about two weeks, during the next full moon," Jack replied.

I gripped my chair, wondering what it meant for me. A feeling bubbled up that I tried to push away as an acidic burning built in my stomach, recalling the words Jasmine had said to me months earlier. *"I know you think Luke is just making up work to stay away from you, but running a pack isn't easy. Maybe if you pitched in sometimes, you'd see how much goes into it."*

Chapter 2

Two weeks passed in a flash, and on a late, chilly evening, I found myself bundled up with Libby seated in my lap in the pack's outdoor stadium. Luke planted himself next to me, a formality for the ceremony—beta seated next to his mate. I think I forgot how to breathe. It had been a month since I'd last seen him.

I can't lie—a part of me was happy he wasn't happy. Maybe all of me was. How could I want him to be happy after how much he'd hurt me? No, he was clearly not happy at all and couldn't hide it from me because when mates were close to each other, we could feel all of each other's emotions.

But still. I missed him.

And I missed him now as he sat down next to me, his warm, comforting scent drifting through the air around me, the cold breeze carrying it toward me.

"Hey," he said as he turned toward me, the moonlight reflecting off his perfectly coiffed hair, his light brown eyes glowing in the darkness. He was nervous. I didn't have to look at his clenched fists to know that.

"Luke," I replied, not able to tear my eyes away from his gentle features, the barely there freckles that dotted his nose, and full lips that I must have kissed a million times—his lips that were practically made for mine.

"How are you, Lucy?"

"Great." I rolled my eyes. But while that may have worked on most people, I knew he could feel everything—the devastation of being so physically close and yet, mentally so far.

"Dada!" Libby cried out, reaching for him. He offered her a quick smile, pulling her into his lap.

Jack and Tyler took their seats in the chairs next to ours, giving us both friendly smiles.

"Congrats again, man." Luke gave Jack a pat on the arm.

"I'm just looking forward to the inauguration sex," Tyler quipped to all of us.

"Sex!" Libby repeated. Luke and I widened our eyes at her while Tyler and Jack burst out laughing.

"Tyler! Look what you've done!" I got up and swatted at him.

"Damn, that just made the night even better!" Tyler chuckled.

"You are never to go near my daughter again!" I glared at him. "Look what you're teaching her!"

"Well, that's one way to get out of babysitting duty." Jack snickered.

"Right?" Tyler added as they shared a wicked smile.

Just then, Blake came on stage with Jasmine, and the crowd quieted. Following them was our temple priest, Bernard, and a man who looked to be about in his midthirties. Blake stepped aside and Bernard took the front of the stage, leading the pack in a chant and then a prayer.

Once the final words of the prayer drifted into the distance, Bernard cleared his throat and ran his eyes along the crowd. "Before we begin tonight's event, I have an announcement to share with the pack. After being your priest for over fifty years, it has finally come time for me to retire. I still fondly recall the day I took my oath. I came to this pack as a young man with dreams to inspire faith in those who were lost, offer wisdom and advice to those in need, and most of all, serve Artemis, the goddess who grants us life and bestows miracles.

"What I did not anticipate was that it would be the reverse. I came to be the one to inspire, and instead, all of you have both humbled and educated me in how unpredictable, difficult, and also how wonderful life can be—how every one of us is at the mercy of Artemis, but when we live by her teachings, we can feel at peace that we have lived a good and honorable life. Throughout my time as priest, I have answered her call over and over again, to help guide my fellow pack members in the direction of good. And I have come along on all your journeys as you have celebrated life, mourned death, and everything in between. To be able to witness these most vulnerable and intimate moments with all of you has truly been a blessing.

"I won't make this speech too long, as I will still be with all of you here in the pack, and there will be plenty of opportunity to speak with everyone tonight before our full moon run. However, it is time to announce my successor." He glanced over his shoulder and gestured for the man standing just behind him to move forward. The man nodded and stepped next to Bernard, who continued, "Colvin will be taking my place tonight and moving forward. He apprenticed at the Oyster Sky Pack in Maine for the past ten years and now comes here with his mate and two daughters, and I have all the faith he will be a wonderful priest for all of you, especially during these changing times."

Did Bernard grimace? While I'd never had anything against him in particular—he always seemed like a pretty nice guy—he also wasn't known for being that open-minded. It still baffled me that he'd allowed Jasmine to get married in the temple while denying Luke the same courtesy.

For his final words, Bernard said, "As his first act as your new priest, he will be leading the ceremony today." He then bowed his head and exited the stage. The temple choir came out as Blake and Jasmine took seats next to our group along with Colvin. They sang a couple songs and the ceremony finally commenced.

As Blake and Jack cut their hands and brought them together to seal the bond, a warmth spread through me, pride for my big brother. Out of all my brothers, he had always been the most caring toward me, and he had also gone through the most as the first openly gay werewolf in our pack. I couldn't help but beam that our alpha was able to overlook that in our ridiculously conservative and religious pack and offer him such a high-ranking position. As much as Blake annoyed me, I couldn't deny he was a good guy. And that sometimes annoyed me more, because I couldn't hate him even though a lot of the time I wanted to. It was no secret that we didn't get along.

After the ceremony ended, Luke gave me a friendly squeeze on the shoulder as I held a sleeping Libby in my arms. "Thanks for sitting up here with me." Gone were the days when he'd wrap me in a hug.

"I'm your mate. Obviously I'm going to sit here with you! That's the beta mate's job, right? To be your good little wifey who shows up to events with you and looks pretty on your arm. That's all you need me for."

"Lucy," Luke breathed out, and the fact that he was becoming irritated was clear as day. Because I wasn't sweet and docile like the person I was sure he wished he'd chosen—his fated mate. I stared at him, and he didn't say anything for a long time. Finally, he let out a sigh and said, "That's not true, Lucy." Then he gave me a pat on the arm and turned to walk away.

Goddess, I wish I could say I was strong and just stuck my middle finger up at him, deciding I was too good for him anyway. But all it did was made me spiral back into that bad place. I couldn't put Libby in her stroller fast enough, shoving the handle right into my mom's hands as soon as I found her.

"Erin!" I called out, as soon as I found my friend. And before anyone could stop me, we were doing shots at the outdoor bar that had been set up for the event. Yeah, I probably should have been on better behavior. After all, this was my brother's night. But all I wanted to do was forget everything I ever felt for Luke, everything I still felt for him—the man who had completely shattered me. And tequila was one thing that never let me down.

Before I knew it, my vision had turned zigzaggy, and my cheeks were warm against the cold breeze of the night. My friends were all hugging each other, declaring our love. But I couldn't push my resentment away. I spotted Luke in the crowd, a smile on his face as he conversed with members of the pack. Fuck him. Fuck him!

I turned and found exactly what I needed. I headed straight for the microphone that was left unsupervised on the stage. My vision was a bit blurry, and I stumbled a few times as I made my way over. It was actually a bit of effort to climb up onto it, but I had long legs, which were necessary at that moment. I soon grasped the microphone in my hand, flicking it on.

"Luke!" I shouted, and everyone who had stayed for the after-party—who would be joining us for the full moon run—quieted, staring up at me. What had been a rambunctious crowd had turned silent.

"Fucking Artemis." I heard Blake's voice in the distance. He was too far to get to me quickly, so I ignored him and continued.

"Luke, if you think I'm here crying over you, I'm not! There are so many men! So many! And they actually satisfy my needs! And you know what else satisfies me better than you? My vibrator! My vibrator that's charged and ready for me at ho—"

Before I had a chance to finish, Jack had his arms wrapped around me. "Stop!" I shouted.

"That's enough, Lucy." Luke was right next to us, pulling the mic from my hand. "How much did you drink?" He wrinkled his nose.

I tried to wriggle free, but Jack kept a good hold, carrying me off the stage. He kept a tight grip on me as he took me away from the celebration. Murmurs echoed around me, and I could sense that everyone's eyes were trained on me. But I was too drunk to care.

Jack carried me all the way to the packhouse with Luke trailing. Then he set me on the living room couch. I looked between the two of them.

"Why did you do that, Lucy?" Jack asked.

"What! Luke deserved it! Deserved to know how great I'm doing without him." I glared at Luke.

"Goddess, she's drunk out of her mind. She can barely speak straight." Luke shook his head. "Goddess, Jack, I'm really sorry about this."

Jack gave Luke's arm a squeeze. "Hey, it's not your fault. It's not like you shoved a bottle down her throat. This is all her own doing."

"Don't talk about me like I'm not here!" I shouted.

"Luce, why don't you sleep it off, okay? Just lie down, and we'll talk about this tomorrow." Jack grabbed a blanket off one of the chairs in the living room.

Luke just continued staring at me, and even though I could barely see straight, I could tell the look he was giving me wasn't good, his anger boiling the blood in my veins. All I could think to say was, "Luke, you're an asshole."

"Just lie down, Lucy." Jack guided me onto a comfortable pillow and threw the blanket he'd grabbed over me. "That's right. Now just sleep it off."

We won't talk about what happened the next morning. We won't talk about how Luke looked at me, like I was the biggest mistake of his life. We also won't talk about how my dad came to collect me to bring me home, disappointment clear as day on his face. We won't even talk about how my parents just sighed as if they knew there was nothing they could say to me, having given up on lecturing me long ago, finding it fruitless now that I was as big of a fuckup as I was.

"Knock knock," Tyler's voice said from behind my closed bedroom door that afternoon.

"Leave me alone," I groaned out.

"We're coming in," Jack said.

"You have ten seconds to make sure all your lady parts are covered," Tyler added. "Trust me, you're way better off putting them behind a paywall anyway. I wish I knew from experience, but Jack's pretty possessive about my man parts." He snickered.

I groaned again, and they walked in and knelt down by my bed.

"So, Lucy, want to talk about what happened last night?" Jack asked, making himself comfortable on the floor by my bed.

"Not particularly," I replied.

"If your goal is to be the Kardashian of Midnight Maple Pack, then last night was perfect." Tyler made an okay sign with his fingers.

I let out a moan.

"So when can we expect the sex tape?" Tyler chuckled.

Jack gave him a look and Tyler covered his mouth, sitting back. Jack then turned to me and said, "Honestly, I don't think I need to lecture you too much, because you've probably humiliated yourself enough."

"Luke deserved it," is all I managed to say.

"I'm pretty sure that the only thing you did to Luke was torture him with secondhand embarrassment."

"I'm not the one who broke up my family."

Jack sighed. "If you're trying to convince Luke he should take you back, that was not the way to do it. As your brother, I'm telling you—get your shit together. The only thing you're doing is making a fool out of yourself and driving Luke further away."

"Sex tape will definitely help." Tyler snickered. "Just kidding. Don't listen to me. Listen to the rational one in the room."

Chapter 3

"Now I know you're definitely going through a crisis," Valerie said as I strolled into the bakery café, where I'd recently been rehired, just before seven thirty. She made a show of looking at her watch and putting her hand on her voluptuous hip. "Early? Really?"

"I'm not that early." I rolled my eyes.

"Compared to your usual seven fifty, this is damn early." She eyed me up and down as I walked past her to drop off my bag and throw on an apron and then took my place at the register.

I went through the usual morning routine, falling right back into it easily even though it had been months since I'd come to work. There was something comforting about it, like meeting up with an old friend after not seeing them for a long time. It was like I'd never left. After the morning rush ended and the place cleared out, I was about to reach for the spray bottle and rag when Valerie broke the silence. "Not a single, *Hi, handsome* or *Hey, good-looking* today?"

"I'm not going through a crisis."

"Your little speech on Tuesday says otherwise."

"So I got a little drunk!" I threw my hands up. "I got a little carried away!"

Valerie crossed her arms, not saying anything.

"Okay, I fucked up," I admitted.

"At least you're admitting it. Probably biggest shock of the day."

"I can admit when I fucked up!" I huffed.

"Really, Lucy? I don't think I recall you ever admitting to fucking up. Even when you forgot to add sugar to all those cookies we made for the spring equinox. When there was no one else it could have possibly been."

I pouted and turned away from her.

"Look, Lucy. I know you. You remind me a lot of me when I was young. But you're not going to get anywhere unless you admit fault sometimes and own up to your mistakes. All you're doing is digging yourself into a bigger pit. And at some point, the hole's going to be too deep to climb out of."

I ignored her and walked into the dining area so I could wipe down the tables. I didn't come here to get lectured. I came here to work and collect a paycheck.

"All I'm saying is, if there's something you want to talk about, I'm here to listen. I know there are plenty of people that are going to gossip and not let you live your little speech down. But I'm not one of those people. I care about you, Lucy."

I sighed, weighing the options in my mind. After I finished wiping down the tables, I switched to sweeping and then worked on the counters. Since no one else was scheduled for a shift today, I was stuck at the front of the house, even though I would have preferred to be prepping dough, getting lost in the flour, eggs, sugar, vanilla extract, chocolate chips . . .

And Luke's emotions that had seared my skin came back to me, his anger and shame flowing through my veins as he stared at me on that packhouse couch. I'd truly fucked up.

"Valerie," I finally said as a tear slipped down my cheek, and I quickly wiped it away.

"Ready to talk?" she asked, coming up front, adjusting the elastic holding her long red hair into a bun, flour dusting her forearms.

I hesitated for a moment. Then I finally let it out. "My mate hates me. He wants nothing to do with me anymore. I don't know what to do." More tears trickled down my cheeks, and I sniffed, knowing my nose was swelling and reddening—not a great look for me.

"I'm sure that's not true. Did he say that to you?"

I shook my head.

"Well, what has he said?"

"That he wishes I'd grow up." I cringed, recalling how many times he'd said it to me, like a broken record. "And stop being selfish."

"Okay, well, you have something to work with then."

"I don't know what to do." I wrapped my arms around myself, full of self-pity, wishing the pain would go away. I hated feeling vulnerable and helpless like this and tried to avoid it as much as I could. When I was forced to admit fault, it tore through me. If I just told myself it wasn't me . . . But I knew I couldn't get away with it anymore. My whole life had been torn apart.

"To be honest, I don't think you're selfish. Well, not completely. You sometimes *do* selfish things. But I think most of the time, you are genuinely trying to be helpful. You just do it in a way that doesn't make sense to the people you're trying to help."

"What do you mean?" I blinked, trying to wrap my head around what Valerie was saying.

"Like, take Talia for example. Why did you try to pair her up with your cousin?"

"Because she told me she didn't want to be with her mate. And I tried to help her find a replacement mate. I was trying to help her."

"And when you were friends with Jasmine, why were you constantly trying to push her to go to parties and drink?"

"Because she was always so stressed. I wanted her to finally let loose and stop being so stressed out all the time."

Valerie nodded. "Here's the problem, Lucy. You were helping them in ways that *you* thought were helpful to them but not considering their feelings, the big picture, and what would *actually* be helpful to them. With Talia, she didn't understand werewolf culture, so she didn't understand that these men would just assume she wanted something casual. With Jasmine, she doesn't like going to parties and drinking. That's not the type of person she is. In fact, I'd say it probably stressed her out even more than anything, because I can only imagine that the whole time she'd have been worrying about what her parents would do if they found out."

I looked down at the ground and sniffed. "So what should I do?" I mumbled.

"Well, why don't you start by trying to improve on that. Start actually considering all the factors before you help someone."

I nodded, staring at the floor, my eyes tracing the black-and-white industrial tiles.

"I'll let you reflect on that while I get back to work," Valerie said, stepping away.

I settled myself by the register. I continued to take orders as customers trickled in, a painful knot in my stomach that wouldn't cease.

And then, it came to me!

"Valerie!" I shouted.

"Yes?" she called from the back.

"I know what I'm going to do!" A smile found its way back to my face.

"What?"

"I'm going to show Luke I've grown up. I'm going to move out of my parents' house."

"Okay, good first step."

"And!"

"And?"

"I'm going to make a list of all the things I'm going to do to prove to Luke that I'm a good, helpful, unselfish person and beta mate material!" My hands shaky with energy pulsing through them, I pulled out some receipt paper and started scribbling on it until I had my list.

1. Help the gays

2. Kick ass at training

3. Potty train Libby

Valerie came out just as I was finishing the last line and looked over my shoulder. "Is Libby even old enough to potty train yet?"

"Probably not, but that's why Luke will be so impressed when I do it!"

Chapter 4

At first, I thought it had worked out perfectly! One of my best friends, Madison, also wanted to move out of her house, especially now that she'd gotten a job at the temple as the admin after old lady Henrietta, the pack gossip queen, retired, following Bernard out the door.

We took over a three-bedroom that was being abandoned by a couple moving into their first house. We agreed I would pay two-thirds of the rent since my daughter would be occupying the second bedroom. I should have honestly put up more of a fight since Libby's bedroom was really more of a closet. There was just enough room to fit her bed and a dresser. But Madison also argued that Luke was still helping support me, so I had a dual income whereas she only had one. So I finally gave in.

I should have known on day one that it was going to be a disaster. Before I was even allowed to move a single one of my items into the place, Madison went all drill sergeant on me and forced me to scrub the place down to an inch of its life.

She inspected every baseboard and every corner. She swept and mopped a second time after I'd done it. She used so much bleach in the bathroom and kitchen my eyes burned. Clearly, she had issues. I mean, we're werewolves for Goddess's sake! It wasn't even like we could get sick. And some of us even sleep outdoors in our wolf form from time to time. Not me personally, of course, but it wasn't uncommon!

And then when I finally began bringing all my kitchen stuff in, she watched me like a hawk, making sure that where I put everything made sense. When I accidentally spilled some flour on the floor and didn't immediately clean it up, you'd think I'd spilled her blood instead. I mean, I'd always known Madison was a bit particular, but I didn't realize the extent.

And, yeah, okay, I wasn't the tidiest person ever. Which Madison made very fucking clear every time she spotted a wrapper outside the trash can or snuck by my room. I mean, okay, Luke was also never a fan of me leaving my clothes around and never putting my makeup away after I used it, or when I'd accidentally leave my curling iron plugged in. But I'd always remind him we had housekeeping, and that usually appeased him enough. But when I brought up the idea of housekeeping to Madison, she promptly asked if I'd be paying.

A few days later, it was my turn with Libby. And if Madison was irritated with me before, now she was full-out raging. "Why are Libby's toys all over the living room?"

"She was playing."

"And why didn't she put them away?"

"Because she had to eat lunch and take a nap."

"And you didn't make sure the room was clean before that?"

"Madison, do you have any idea how much work it is just to get her into the kitchen to eat? And put her down for a nap? You want me to also make sure all of her toys are put away?"

"Obviously! Look at what a mess she made!"

I sighed and rolled my eyes. "No."

"What do you mean, no?"

"I pay more rent for this apartment, so I get majority rule. If you don't like the toys, you pick them up." With that, I stomped away. It was my day off from work. I wasn't going to spend it cleaning. And I should have known what was coming next when Madison stepped in the kitchen—

"Lucy!"

"Dear Goddess, what?"

"There's food residue everywhere. You didn't even bother to wipe anything down after Libby ate. And is that a bowl and fork in the sink? Why didn't you wash them after you were done?"

"I'm going to take a nap," I replied.

After I got out of work the next day, I found Jasmine and Tyler in the packhouse, as I'd expected after checking the packhouse calendar that I still had access to. "I'm here for the Social Development Committee meeting."

They both looked up at me, tilting their heads.

"This is where you meet about the gay stuff, right?"

"The gay stuff?" Jasmine questioned, blinking a few times.

"Yeah! I want to help the gays!" I replied, dragging the big, comfortable reading chair Jasmine had in the corner of her office over to where she and Tyler were seated at her desk.

"Lucy, what are you doing here?" Jasmine asked.

"What does it look like? I'm getting involved with pack leadership and pitching in."

"Oh. Kay." Jasmine sat back, a blank look on her face.

"Anyway, I came prepared. I wrote out a list of ideas for changes we can make around the pack to make it more welcoming."

Tyler crossed his arms and leaned back in his chair. "Okay, let's hear them."

I dug into my purse, pulled out a piece of paper, unfolded it, and cleared my throat. "Okay, idea number one is we should have a gay pride parade."

"A gay pride parade?" Tyler asked. "And who exactly would attend the parade?"

"I mean, you'd go, right?"

"Yeah, sure." Tyler nodded. "But one person isn't going to make a whole parade."

"All the other gays would go too."

"Can you please stop calling them 'the gays'?" Jasmine blurted out. "It's so insensitive."

"Isn't that what they are?"

Tyler chuckled. "Stick with LGBTQ+."

I took a deep breath. "Okay, sorry. LGBTQ+."

Tyler smiled. "I appreciate the enthusiasm for a parade. But I'm not sure the community or the pack is ready for one. That's not to say we can't get there one day, but just knowing the people who this parade would be for, they're not ready to be out and proud in front of the pack yet. But I will float your idea by some of them, just in case I'm wrong about that."

I let out a breath. "Okay."

"Don't lose hope. Looking forward to seeing you and Libby in your matching rainbow outfits once we do have one." He gave me an encouraging wink. "Knowing you, it'll be everything. I saw the outfit from boobgate. You'll definitely make my gay heart proud." He gave my arm a squeeze.

I ignored his comment and looked down at my list again. "I have more ideas." I straightened up. "I was thinking we could build a gay bar."

"Where would we build it, and how much would it cost?" Jasmine asked.

"In the downtown area. And I don't know. But we have pack funds we can use, right?"

"On what land in the downtown area? All of the houses and buildings are already super close together because there's no land."

"Couldn't we tear something down or renovate something? Like relocate someone to another house?"

"Why don't we table this idea as something more long-term?" Tyler offered. "Maybe once you can come back to us with a more solid plan for how this would work, including what land we'd use, how much it would cost the pack, who would run it, what you think the average occupancy on any given night would be, etcetera, etcetera. I like the idea of a safe space, but I'm not sure that a bar that everyone in the pack knows about is quite right."

I pressed my lips together, but I wouldn't be discouraged. "All right, well idea three is for Jack to tell the pack his coming out story."

"Did Jack agree to that?"

I shrugged. "Well, no, but he will once I talk to him."

Tyler smiled and shook his head like he was laughing at some inside joke. "Really, your brother? Speak publicly? About the one thing he's the most insecure about?"

I slumped my shoulders. "I'm just trying to help. I tried to think of things that could help the ga—the LGBTQ+ people. I really want to help."

Tyler gave my shoulder a squeeze. "You need to think smaller scale. Two of your ideas are super grand, and the other is making someone else do your work for you. Try to think of small steps we can take. Like, for example, the rainbow stickers have been a huge hit. A lot of people have been super supportive, putting stickers on their windows, which has shown everyone that there's a bigger group of allies in the pack than we initially thought. We need more stickers for now, until we're all finally ready to bust out of the closet with Cher on full blast."

Chapter 5

So, how hard could potty training possibly be? I mean, every parent does it, right? And everyone seems to graduate. Even my brother Mark, who was never the sharpest tool in the shed, got potty trained. With that as her bar, Libby should be a genius at this.

It all started so well. I went out and bought a super cute pink potty with a unicorn on it. Libby loved it as soon as she saw it. We practiced by sitting on it. I read something somewhere about leaving your toddler naked, and they'd know to use the potty since they'd realize they weren't wearing a diaper. I was already well on my way to having Libby potty trained. It was late fall heading into winter, so I just blasted the heat. Madison was out anyway, so she wouldn't be able to complain about bills or whatever else she wanted to complain about.

Okay, so clearly Libby didn't make the connection between not wearing a diaper and using the potty. It was pretty obvious when I found the huge wet stain on the living room carpet that I then spent way too long cleaning because I didn't want to hear from Madison about how there was piss all over the floor.

We won't talk about what else happened that day. Let's just say, day one of potty training was a big fail. I slipped a diaper back on Libby before I put her pajamas on and put her to bed. It's okay, one bad day didn't mean it wouldn't happen. I'd just have to do a better job reading through all of the potty training information. To be fair, I had just skimmed it.

After I read a bedtime story to Libby and tucked her in, I came back out to the living room to find Madison sneaking into the apartment long after she normally came home from work. "And where have you been?"

"Oh, hey," Madison replied, and I didn't fail to notice that her cheeks were tinted pink. Hmm. "Just a long day at work."

"I hope you're getting paid overtime."

"Something like that."

She continued walking to her room. Fortunately, whatever she had been up to had left her so preoccupied she didn't bother to give me her nightly lecture about everything that was out of place. I couldn't help but notice Libby's shoes sprawled out on the entryway floor, not put away in the closet like Madison demanded.

I guess I shouldn't have celebrated too early, because—

Madison screamed from her bedroom, "Lucy!"

I let out a sigh. "What now?"

"Why is there *poop* on my bedroom floor?"

Oh shit. I ran over, and I couldn't help but almost burst out laughing because it was all over Madison's sock after she'd clearly stepped in it. I tried my best to stifle my laughter, but still a little got out.

"It's not fucking funny!" Oh shit. Madison almost never swore, so she was clearly pissed. "Goddess, I should have known. I could smell it before I even walked in and couldn't figure out why! Again, why is there *poop* in my bedroom?"

"I started potty training Libby."

"And what, is my bedroom her *potty*?"

"Well, it wasn't supposed to be but now that you mention it . . ."

"Fucking Artemis, Lucy! I am seriously regretting moving in with you." She pulled her sock off, and before I could process what she was doing, she threw it in my face.

"Hey!" I scrunched my nose, almost gagging from the shit now on my face.

"This is your mess. So clean it! I'm going to take a shower!" Madison walked away toward her bathroom.

I went to my own bathroom first to clean my face, and then got to work scrubbing Madison's carpet. I'd honestly thought I'd gotten every accident in the house. But I guess I must have missed one crucial spot. I can't lie though—it was pretty satisfying seeing

Madison step in Libby's shit after she'd been harassing me about keeping a clean place all that time.

I was just finishing up when Madison returned from her shower, wrapped in a bathrobe.

"I didn't realize there was so much work at the temple they need you to work overtime," I commented.

"Well, if you must know," Madison started in a very pompous sort of way, "Cole's been teaching me all about Artemis's scriptures and showing me all new ways to look at so many of the teachings and stories."

"Cole?"

"Yes, Colvin, whatever. I call him Cole. He's actually really intelligent. I could just listen to him for hours. Today we went over some of her hunting stories, how they are important to us as werewolves. Artemis loves to hunt and punishes harshly anyone who crosses her. And because she gifted a piece of her spirit to werewolves, it is in our nature to do so as well."

"Bore me to hell," I responded.

"Well, I find it very interesting." She rolled her eyes, and took a seat at her vanity, combing out her hair. "I wouldn't expect someone who's a sinner to care."

"Who are you calling a sinner?"

"Please, Lucy. You called yourself out the other night when you told the whole pack you've been sleeping around. And it's not exactly a secret that you and Luke weren't allowed to get married in the temple. I personally don't care what you do. But at least own up to it."

"That's coming from someone that's apparently staying after work to hang out with *Cole*?" I scoffed. "Last I checked he's married and our *priest*."

"It's not like that. We just enjoy having intellectual discussions about our deity. Anyway, if it's all right, I'd like to get dressed for bed now. Can you get out of my room?"

I rolled my eyes, and walked out, closing her door behind me. Goddess, help me survive the next however long with Madison. I didn't know how much longer I'd be able to take it.

Chapter 6

Okay, so my ideas for how to help the LGBTQ+ community in our pack weren't exactly appreciated as much as I thought they would be. And potty training was kind of a flop so far. But I still had one part of my list going for me—well, maybe.

I'd been kind of banking on doing so well at the other two things that I could sort of slack on this last one. The thing was, even though I came from a long line of warriors, training was just not my thing. I mean, how did people actually enjoy gasping for air, getting runner's cramps, and being so sore you couldn't even properly use the toilet the next day?

But now this was my last chance to really shine, and I knew that my skipping out on training had been a real sticking point for Luke. How could he possibly understand? I mean, he likes that shit. He'd probably spend the entire day at the gym lifting those metal pole thingies with the weights on them if he could. He used to do fifty push-ups before bed and as soon as he woke up every morning as a routine. He volunteered to lead the elementary school training as extra on top of everything else he was already doing. Which was quite convenient for him when it came to splitting up our parenting schedules.

I sighed and rang the doorbell to Emma and Kyle's house. We'd agreed to meet up that day to do each other's nails and let our kids play with each other.

"Lucy! Come on in!" Emma greeted me with a hug. "No Madison today?"

"Nah, she has work," I replied, maneuvering Libby's stroller into the house. I quickly pulled her out to give her free rein to play with her cousins.

"I feel like Madison's always working lately."

"Works out great for me. Don't have to listen to all her nagging."

"I mean, I knew Madison was a little high maintenance, but I didn't realize she was that bad."

"Oh, she's bad!" I followed Emma into the living room where we got comfortable on the floor, next to the coffee table.

"What color are you thinking this week?" she asked, pulling out her clear baggy filled to the brim with different polishes.

"Let's do purple. Dark purple."

"Moody!"

"Yeah, well, why shouldn't I be?" As I said that, we heard a large crash and turned to find our pups had knocked over a bunch of blocks. No one seemed to be hurt, so we turned back to what we were doing.

"Still nothing from Luke? Honestly, I think he misses you, Lucy." Emma took my hand in hers and began applying a clear bottom coat.

"Well, he sure doesn't show it."

"I mean, you did kind of tell him you were screwing a whole bunch of other guys." She snickered and elbowed me. "Not sure I'd want to talk to Kyle if he announced to the whole pack that he was getting around with some other mystery girls."

"He deserved it." All my muscles tensed. I had to force myself not to clench my hands into fists since Emma was currently painting them.

"Does he really though?"

"Why wouldn't he?"

"I mean, Lucy, he's always been a good mate to you, a good dad to Libby. Right? Even when he had a fated mate, he still chose you."

"But what about when I was depressed? And I told him I needed more of his support?"

"He got you a nanny, didn't he?"

But I needed him. I needed my mate. I needed his affection. I needed him to hold me and tell me everything would be okay. I needed his love. I needed him to spend time with Libby and me as a family and not just delegate all his responsibilities to others so he could spend more time working.

"That's not the point."

"Lucy, sometimes I just don't get you."

Luke doesn't get me either. Does anyone get me?

I sat back in reflection as Emma continued to paint my nails. After my nails dried, we fed our pups and put them down for naps, and then I worked on Emma's hands. I carefully painted each one of her nails light pink, her usual choice of color. So unoriginal.

Just as her nails were drying, my brother Kyle walked in, instantly pulling his mate in for a kiss. She returned his affection with an intimate embrace, careful so her nails wouldn't touch him. He then turned to me and gave me a quick hug.

"How are the pups?" Kyle asked.

"Still napping," Emma replied. "But they should be waking soon. I'll go check on them." She exited the room.

"Kyle, I need to ask you for a big favor." I gave my brother my winning smile.

"Oh, Goddess. What is it now? I hope we don't have to do another sleepover with Libby. You know what happened last time."

"Kyle, you totally made that up." I pushed on his arm.

"No, she was really creepy. I went to check in on her and Ethan at night, and she was just staring at the corner of the room with her big, sinister eyes, didn't even acknowledge me, and then waved to the corner and said, 'bye bye.' When I asked her who she said 'bye

bye' to, she just giggled in a really disturbing way and closed her eyes."

"What kind of warrior are you, being terrified of a baby?" I gave him a playful shove.

"A creepy baby that sees ghosts. And possibly summons them."

"You've been watching too many horror movies."

"I saw what I saw."

"Okay, whatever. Anyway, that's not the favor I need. I need you and Jack to train me."

"To train you?"

"Yes, train me to spar. I want to get really good."

He looked me up and down. "You, Lucy Hemming, want to get really good at sparring?"

"Yes."

"Did Libby summon a ghost to possess you or something?"

"What?"

"I thought that getting out of sparring was your thing. Now you want to get in to sparring?"

"I've decided to make some positive changes in my life."

He crossed his arms and didn't say anything.

"Come on! You and Jack are both really good warriors!"

His mouth lifted in the corners. "Yeah, we are really good. Which means we're both busy. But I know two guys who aren't too busy and can't say no to our orders."

"Who?"

"Mark and Neil."

"Mark and Neil?" I shrieked. "Our little brothers?"

"Mark and Neil are perfect. They've got all the main sparring moves down, and they're still fresh as warriors, so it'll be good for them to train someone else."

I knew I probably shouldn't agree. But, well, I was desperate to prove myself, and beggars can't be choosers.

Yep, I knew I should have never agreed. This was a bad, bad idea.

I was complete shit at training, and Mark and Neil both took full advantage.

First, they made me run four laps around the indoor track. Every time I tried to slow down, they'd shout at me. "Pick it up!" When I got around the second lap and tried to slow to a walk, they both came up on either side of me and grabbed my elbows, forcing me back into a run. By the time I finally finished the fourth lap, my chest was tight and my lungs were making barking noises.

"Okay, let's get to work." Mark clapped his hands.

"Don't I get a water break?" I whined, still trying to catch my breath, my heart beating so fast I was sure it was going to beat right out of my chest.

"You said you wanted to kick ass at training, right?" Mark gave me a dubious look as if he were trying to call my bluff. And then everything burned through my memories, everything that had gone down since I'd found out that Luke and Jasmine were mates. All our fights, all the profound silence between us, the way he was constantly comparing me to her—even if it wasn't outright, I could just tell. Then the way I sank into a depression, the constant uphill battle to be a good mate and mother while holding on to my sanity, getting kicked out of the packhouse, and then everything I'd said in front of the pack. Those words that I knew would always haunt me. It was clear in the looks people gave me when I passed them by, and when I saw people whispering and glancing my way.

"I'm in it to win it!" I declared, pulling myself together. I was going to do this!

They both raised their eyebrows. Okay, they didn't believe in me. But I was a fighter. I could do this.

And of course they weren't planning to go easy on me. First, they made me do twenty-five push-ups. I was able to get about two good ones in before I had to switch to my knees, which thankfully they didn't berate me for. I groaned and moaned, forcing myself through each one, my arms and shoulders burning. Then, with no break in between, they had me do a series of mountain climbers, walking lunges across the gym floor, and bicycle crunches.

"Okay, now you should be good at this one." Neil pulled out a bench as I panted, gulping down water. "Twenty squats. Butt to the bench."

"Why would I be any better at this one than the other ones?" I narrowed my eyes at him.

"Well, all the boyfriends you told Luke and the pack about. Sounds like you've had practice. Just not at the gym."

"You asshole!" I yelled, pushing on his chest. "You're just jealous because your only girlfriend is Palm Solo!"

Mark snickered. "Good one, sis!" He gave me a high five. "Okay, seems like you're ready for some sparring."

"Let's go. Ready to kick both your asses!" I bounced from foot to foot. Okay, they could definitely both kick my ass without even trying, but I was fired up now.

We began the sparring portion of the session with different punches. At first, they'd act serious, but then they'd start playing around. I tried to punch Mark, and he grabbed my arm, effortlessly flipping me onto his shoulders and running around while I tried to get off and the two of them laughed at me.

Next, I went at it with Neil, throwing out different types of punches as he called them out. When I wasn't expecting it, he grabbed my hand and pulled me into a headlock.

"Noogie noogie noogie." Neil chuckled as he messed up my hair with his knuckles.

"Hey!" I got up once he let me go and sorted out my hair. "Stop it!"

They both laughed at me.

"Come on, we're stuck training a newb. You have to let us have a little fun," Neil teased.

"I'm not a newb."

They side-eyed each other. Okay, even though I was older than them, clearly, I was a newb. Could you blame me? Why would anyone want to do this when they had the fine excuse of period cramps to just sit on the sidelines and check out all the good-looking guys in our training class instead? When I was growing up, it was even better because all the trainers were male. So they never questioned the fact that my period essentially never stopped.

Mark got into a defensive stance. "Okay, come on, Luce. Basic kicks. Left leg. Front kick!" he shouted as I kicked forward, and he dodged it. "Side kick!" I went again. Then, "Round kick!" I pushed off my back leg, bringing my knee up, and pivoted, landing the perfect kick against Mark's hand as he stopped me.

"Nice. Now donkey kick!"

"What?" I squinted at him.

They both gave each other looks, hopped onto their hands and kicked back like donkeys, just nearly missing my chin. I screamed and fell backward onto my ass.

They both got up and laughed. "Kyle was right, this is fun." Neil clutched at his stomach.

The session continued like that. First, they'd start serious and then do something to tease me. In the end, I was forcing myself not to cry, not wanting them to know how much they got to me. I was their big sister for Goddess's sake!

Once the bell rang, signaling lunchtime, I fell back onto a mat, defeated. They both walked off together, leaving me behind.

I was just about to get up and go wallow in my misery in the shower when a familiar scent drifted into my nose. I looked up to see Luke approaching me and scrambled to my forearms.

"Lucy." He stared down at me. "What are you doing on the ground?"

I let out a deep breath. I'm sure he could feel everything I felt anyway, so what was the sense of hiding it anymore? I brought my knees to my chest and replied, "I was training."

"Here, let me help you up." He held his hand out to me. I reached for it and he pulled me up with minimal effort, as if I weighed nothing. He heaved me toward his body to steady me, and I couldn't help but indulge in the sensations that floated through me. The calming sparks and his sweet, musky scent I'd come to crave like a drug. "Training, huh?" He gave me a look, but I could tell it wasn't accusatory. This had been such a pain point between us during the final months before we'd separated.

I sighed, giving myself some space from him. As much as I wanted to dig my heels in and be tough, show him I was better off without him, I knew that wasn't true. In the end, I wanted him to come back to me, and for us to be a family again. I swallowed my pride and said, "Luke, I'm sorry for the night of Jack's gamma ceremony. The stuff I said wasn't true. There's no one else. The reason I'm training is to show you I can be a good beta mate. And I've been doing other stuff too, like trying to help Jasmine and Tyler with their social committee and potty training Libby to show I care about being a good mom to her."

"Wow, Lucy." He pulled my hands into his and rubbed his fingers along my palms the way he used to, and suddenly it felt like things were back to how they had been. "Honestly, I've missed you," he said, letting out a sigh and planting his head on my shoulder. "I hate how things between us turned out."

I breathed in his scent, and all the memories of how good things had once been between us flooded back in.

"Lucy, would you—would you maybe want to go out to dinner one night? I'll ask my mom to babysit Libby, and maybe we can talk."

"I'd love that."

Chapter 7

It was Luke's turn with Libby on the day of our date, so I rushed directly home to my apartment after I was done with my café shift instead of picking her up from the nanny like I normally would. Madison, unsurprisingly, wasn't home. It was for the best. I didn't have to hear her pester me about kicking my boots off and not putting them away neatly into the closet, or the fact that I'd just flung my hat onto the entryway table instead of putting it in the special hat bin.

I went through my full ritual of getting ready, which started with a half hour hair treatment. Then I shaved every bit of hair off my body, exfoliated myself up and down, and moisturized every last inch of skin. I blew out and curled my hair and then spent copious amounts of time applying a flawless no-makeup makeup look.

I must have pulled out at least fifty dresses before I settled on a bordeaux sweater dress that was the perfect balance of modest and slutty. It covered my arms and was long on my legs, ending at my midcalves, while simultaneously being skintight and dipping low enough to practically show the lace push-up bra I'd donned underneath.

For a final touch, I pulled out a pair of Louboutin So Kates I'd saved up for for several months a few years back. I didn't wear them often since I was already just shy of five-ten, thanks to my freakishly tall family, and they weren't even close to the most comfortable pair of shoes I owned. But Luke was one of the few people who still managed to be taller than me in these heels, and I couldn't deny how hot they looked when I put them on. Tonight was very important. It was definitely a Louboutin kind of night!

At seven, I'd just finished dabbing the slightest bit of perfume onto my wrists, behind my ears, and inside my cleavage, and posting a few selfies onto Instagram for good measure, when the buzzer sounded. I slipped on my pea coat and the crossbody YSL purse that Luke had gifted me as a push present—after I'd talked him into it—and headed downstairs to meet him at the entrance to the apartment building.

Although I was at a confidence level of one hundred after the hours of work I'd put in to look hot AF, my heart still skipped a beat and my legs were a bit shaky as I caught a glimpse of Luke through the glass door to the building. He had clearly spent a good amount of time on his hair as it was perfectly coiffed, and in his hand, he was clutching a bouquet of roses. It had been ages since Luke had brought me flowers. And suddenly hope bloomed in my chest that maybe things weren't truly over for us and could be repaired.

As soon as I pushed the front door open and stepped outside, all of Luke's emotions flooded my body. I could instantly tell he was nervous, but also—was that . . . ? Was he *aroused*? I hadn't sensed him feel that particular way in who knows how long, and tears almost flooded my eyes.

I didn't even know how it happened. Before we had Libby, we had been at it all the time, like rabbits. When he was away from the pack for two years, and I'd rarely see him, we'd spend every second together naked. At first, it was doing everything but. Then after my eighteenth birthday, when we discovered we weren't mates and I finally lost my virginity, I'm pretty sure he spent every second he could inside me.

But then after Libby, it all changed. At first, I didn't feel like it. While werewolves could be back at it within a week due to our speedy healing, I just couldn't get in the mood. Libby cried all the time, and my body wasn't like it was before. While Luke was always super understanding, I could tell it began to eat away at our closeness. And I began to wonder, without the physical aspect of our relationship, did we even have one?

Over time, we slowly began to reconnect. But it wasn't the same. Both of us were constantly arguing and picking fights with each other. And Libby kept crying. All the time. Nonstop. I had always imagined myself being the image of an exemplary beta mate and mom, and suddenly it just felt impossible. And then, one day, Luke just stopped wanting to have sex with me.

I blinked a few times, glancing up into his light brown eyes. Something in him had definitely shifted. He was now looking at me like he used to, before everything went south. "Wow, Lucy, you look amazing," he said, gently taking my hand.

"Thanks," I replied, feeling a bit shy and unsure. "You don't look so bad yourself." His eyes crinkled as he cracked a really sweet smile and tugged on my hand to pull me toward his car.

He brought me over to the passenger side and opened the door for me. Once we were both settled in our seats, I asked, "So where are we going tonight?"

"They just opened a small wine and cheese bar in the casino. It took over the old taproom that wasn't doing that well."

"I'm surprised. Isn't that what tourists usually want after a hike?"

"I think there was too much competition in the area, and the prices were too high for what it was. At least that's what management told us. They're giving this new concept a go. They're sourcing mostly local cheeses and wines. I think you'll like it. Figured we could try it out together and maybe you can give your two cents to management." Luke glanced my way and gave me a heartwarming smile. He did always have one of the best smiles.

When we arrived, I was pleasantly surprised by the place. It was actually really adorable. They'd done the whole place up in a French style, with marble and gold and pops of pink. We were instantly seated at a small table that reminded me of one you'd see at a French café.

"Good evening, Mr. and Mrs. Hemming," the restaurant manager greeted us. "Tonight we have the 2020 Celestial Louise from the local Shelburne Vineyard to offer you." He made eye contact with me and continued, "Mr. Hemming said you're a fan of sparkling wine?"

"Yes, I love sparkling wine!" I exclaimed.

"Perfect, I'll bring a bottle over. On the house, of course."

After he came back, poured us some wine, and took our orders, Luke and I clinked our glasses together and took sips of our wine. "Delicious," I breathed out. "We should go to this vineyard and get some bottles."

Luke smiled and leaned forward. "Lucy, thanks for agreeing to come out to dinner with me. It's nice hanging out with you again. And I know I already told you, but you look so beautiful tonight."

"Must be all the training I've been doing." I winked, wanting to remind him I was trying now.

"Thank you, Lucy. I know you don't enjoy it, but it really means a lot to me that you're trying. Besides the importance of upholding our pack standards in your position as my mate, I also want you to be able to defend yourself if it ever comes down to it. We try our best to keep battles off pack land, but it can happen. And I have to think about you and Libby if that ever goes down."

I was moved by Luke's speech and how much he cared about the small family we'd formed. Goddess, maybe I should have thought more about his insistence on training past how much I hated it. Again, that familiar gross feeling began to form in my stomach, and I pushed it away, turning my mind to other things.

Soon they brought over a huge cheese and charcuterie board for us to share along with a number of appetizers from the chef. We took more sips of our wine, and the conversation turned more lighthearted. It was like things had never changed between us. It was just Luke and me and how we were together before everything bad happened.

Luke ordered another bottle of wine once we polished off the first, and both of us were buzzed. I breathed in the love in the air and the feeling of being floaty and free. Luke took my hand in his, and gentle sparks traveled up and down my arm.

"So how's the apartment?" Luke asked.

"Horrible," I replied. "Madison has some serious issues. I thought you were bad with needing the bed made every day and your obsession with keeping all the bottles turned a certain way. But Madison is literally the clean police. She is on my ass every single second about something that I didn't put away."

Luke snickered. "Sounds like a match made in hell."

"It's the worst, Luke! And Libby's just a baby. But she's on her ass too about her toys and books!"

"To be fair, you are pretty bad about putting things away."

"But she doesn't have to get on my case every second she's home."

Luke rubbed my palm, instantly calming me.

"Maybe I should move back into the packhouse," I suggested, my buzz giving me the courage to broach the subject.

Luke instantly stopped and moved his hand away, and it suddenly felt cold and abandoned. He blinked a few times and then finally replied, "I'm sorry, Lucy. I'm not ready for that yet. I think this was a good first step in rebuilding what we had. But you hurt me a lot, and I'm not ready to let you back in yet. I'm going to need more time."

Part of me wanted to scream at him. Sure, I'd done some hurtful things. But it's not like he was completely innocent either. He'd also broken me. I thought back—most of the terrible things I did were in reaction to him. It first started with him hiding the fact that my best friend was his mate. After we'd been together for four years! And then after that got resolved, other problems started. And instead of listening to my pain, he'd just brush it off as me being needy and whiny. He never once validated any of my feelings.

I needed my mate. If not him, who was going to help me when things felt too overwhelming and impossible with Libby? But he had his job and his duties and always an excuse ready for why his time was more important than mine.

But I'd said all that to him, a million times. And it never went anywhere. So I forced myself to stay silent and instead allow the now familiar ache to pierce my chest. I had two choices—try to live without my mate or continue what I'd begun doing and prove to Luke I was worthy of being his mate. Both options somehow seemed wrong. But I wasn't sure what else I could possibly do at this point. We'd marked each other. Our bond had been made permanent, for better or for worse.

Chapter 8

"Lucy, I'm here for an intervention! Let me in!" My brother-in-law Tyler's voice sounded from the telecom.

I rolled my eyes and buzzed him in. Moments later, he was at my doorstep.

"What did I do now?" I let out an exaggerated sigh, crossing my arms as he stepped past me into the apartment.

"Look, I know you call Libby your pup, but there are some major differences between her and a dog."

"What!" I screeched.

"Okay, so there are times that she's on all fours. And she does sometimes make howling noises. Which I definitely think she gets from your side of the family." He snickered to himself as if he were laughing at an inside joke. "Based solely on my personal experience with Jack making the same kinds of noises."

"Ew! Gross! Tyler!" I yelled, pushing on him. "I literally do not need to know what my brother sounds like in bed! Goddess! You and Emma both! So disgusting!"

"I didn't say he made them in bed. That was your mind going straight there."

"I've never heard Jack make any noise that sounds like Libby howling."

"Okay, he did it on the couch."

"Tyler!" I pushed him again. "If you're going to talk to me about your sex life, then you need to get the fuck out of here!"

He chuckled. "Okay, I'll stop."

"Did you just come here to make me gag?" I folded my arms across my chest and glared at him.

"I'm pretty sure that Libby's already got that covered with her using your apartment as her own personal toilet." He then flopped down on the couch. "Come, sit." He patted the cushion next to him.

I was about to say something when he continued, "Pro tip, you have to bring the pup outside to potty. That way they don't go all over your floor."

I groaned. "Goddess, how did you even find out about that?"

"The usual way. Madison told Emma, Emma told Kyle, and Kyle told Jack. And then Jack laughed about it for hours as he kept making jokes about you using Libby as your own personal revenge tool against Madison for daring to ask you to put your dishes away."

"First of all, Madison does more than just ask me to put my dishes away! And second of all, Libby hasn't been that bad. There have just been a few accidents."

"So Madison didn't step in one of Libby's turds?"

I couldn't help myself from laughing.

"Okay, so that happened," I admitted. "But only once!"

"Libby! Liberate me from Madison's oppression! Release the feces!"

I tried to keep a straight face.

"Libby! Forget hide-and-seek. Instead, let's play take a leak."

I scrunched up my nose, forcing myself not to laugh.

"Duck, duck, set your stool loose."

I'm not going to laugh. I'm not going to laugh.

"Red rover, red rover, Libby, defecate all over."

Not funny, not funny.

"Simon says, get out your rump. Simon says, take a dump."

"Okay, that's enough!" I let out a laugh, unable to hold it in anymore. "I get it!"

Tyler chuckled. "Why are you potty training Libby anyway? Isn't she a bit young to start?"

"That's why Luke will be so impressed once she is! And, anyway, I read plenty of articles about toddlers getting potty trained at eighteen, nineteen months. I think Libby is finally hitting her stride." I took a seat next to him.

"Why will Luke be so impressed with Libby getting potty trained now?" He turned his knees toward me and leaned in.

"Because it'll show him what a great mom I am."

He gave me a half smile and crossed his arms, leaning back a bit. After a beat, he said, "Lucy, I don't think that that's what's going to impress Luke. I think he'd be more impressed if you did things that showed some of the good qualities moms have. When people talk about good moms, they don't talk about how quickly they train their kids to do this or that. They talk about how patient, caring, and selfless they are."

I stared at him, not sure how to respond.

"Like think about your own mom. I'm sure she has better things to do than watch Libby, Ethan, and Miles, but she's always taking them in when you're in a pinch. And when Luke kicked you out of the packhouse, she let you come back home, no questions asked. She didn't blame you for anything and was such a good grandma to Libby even though she throws tantrums all the time. She never once made you feel like you or Libby were being a burden on her."

I bit my lip, realizing Tyler was right. My mom was always so caring to every one of her pups and grandpups. Even though we were never anywhere close to rich growing up, my mom always made sure we had everything we needed. She went without if it meant we went with.

"Instead, why don't you do something that will show Luke how caring you also are. Do something that will be helpful to the pack. Like, why don't you offer to babysit Ryker and Aria one night so Blake and Jasmine can have a date night?"

I scrunched my nose.

"Why not?" Tyler asked.

I sighed. I was too embarrassed to tell Tyler that I thought Luke still harbored feelings for Jasmine. The thing is, it still stung—the whole thing. Sometimes I'd finally start to get over it. But then I'd remember the abrupt slap across my face when I smelled Jasmine all over Luke and he admitted to me that my best friend—my best friend since kindergarten who I trusted with my life—was his mate. That the two of them had hidden it from me and gone behind my back and hooked up without even telling me. And then Jasmine acted as if I was wrong to be upset about the whole thing, as if she hadn't broken friend code.

I knew Luke chose me in the end, and then Jasmine saved his life. So without her, I would have lost my mate forever. And I started to get over it. But it was the way he looked at her sometimes, and the way I could tell he wished I was more like her. They say the Moon Goddess sends you exactly your type, and now it was clear as day who Luke's type really was.

But then a part of me realized Tyler was right. Luke always went on and on about how everyone was overwhelmed with pack leadership duties. It was why they'd brought Jack on. And yeah, I knew for a fact that Jasmine and Blake had plenty of options to watch their kids. They had their parents, their grandparents, and Jack and Tyler who took them in sometimes. But still, it was a gesture. A good one at that. It would show Luke I wanted to help and that I was getting over my issues with Jasmine. And that I could play nice with Blake.

I sighed. "I guess I could do that."

He patted my shoulder. "Of course you can. Give people something to talk about other than your boobs and vibrator. And Libby's shit."

Chapter 9

Early Saturday morning, I dropped Libby off at the packhouse before my shift so Luke could watch her until the nanny got in. We'd worked out the schedule so that he'd go to the gym from five to seven in the morning, be home by seven fifteen when I'd drop Libby off before work, and have her until nine when the nanny got in. Then, if it was my turn with Libby, I'd pick her up at five or earlier. If it was Luke's turn, then I'd go home without her.

A lot of the time, it wasn't even Luke who greeted me at the front door. Whoever happened to answer would take Libby off my hands. But today I was surprised Luke was waiting when I arrived.

"Hey." He smiled—his perfect movie star smile.

"Hey."

"How's it going?"

"Fine, just heading to work."

"I didn't see you on the sparring schedules during the next two-week rotation. Is that because you're working with your brothers now instead? I can note it so no one gets on your case."

I rolled my eyes. "Luke, you're the only one who ever gets on my case. Pretty sure Blake has an allergic reaction every time he has to talk to me. And Jasmine resents the air I breathe. Though, I guess you have Jack to sic on me now."

He chuckled. "Okay, well, then, I'll note it so Jack won't get on your case."

I slumped my shoulders.

"Is something wrong?" he asked. "I can sense that you're anxious."

I sighed. "Honestly, I don't want to train with my brothers anymore."

"Why not?"

"They're my baby brothers, and they kicked my ass! Do you know what it's like for your baby brothers to kick your ass?"

"Yeah, I totally get it. My big sisters kick my ass all the time," he said with a dry sarcasm. "So does my almost sixty-five-year-old dad."

I chuckled at the visual. Luke's dad was in good shape, especially for his age. He still helped run the pack, but a lot less than he had when he had been the beta. I knew that he reasoned with Blake when necessary. He had honed his skills over years of dealing with Blake's dad, whom I'd heard had been a hundred times worse. Blake also sometimes had a temper, but Luke said it was nowhere close to as bad as Alpha James's had been.

"Hey, if you want, I'd be happy to train you," Luke offered. I looked up into his eyes, and I couldn't immediately tell if the warmth that was spreading through my body was me sensing Luke's emotions or if it was my own, our feelings melding together. It had become so infrequent that we were in close proximity to each other that I'd almost forgotten how close we had once been—the mate bond binding us together until we became almost one and the same.

And that was why tearing the bond apart was so unnatural and painful. It was the reason why I had so much difficulty existing beyond it. But now, it felt magical and comforting again.

"Yeah, I'd like that," I replied.

"How about tomorrow? I don't work as much on Sundays. I could train you in the afternoon if you'd like. Maybe my mom can watch Libby for a couple hours."

"Yeah, sure. I get off work at four tomorrow."

"See you at the warrior gym at four thirty tomorrow then." He gave me another smile and his eyes seemed to sparkle a bit this time.

The next day, I met Luke at the warrior gym in my turquoise leggings and sports bra set. I'd been told it brought out my eyes before, and I thought it would be good to wear for this occasion.

The gym was mostly empty when I arrived. Warriors didn't generally train on Sundays and Mondays and only worked if they had patrol duty on those two days. There were a few people who had come in on their day off to get their workout in, but I could probably count them all on my fingers.

Luke was waiting for me on a workout bench, phone in his hand, when I walked in. He stood up, smiled, and shook his head as I approached. "You wouldn't be Lucy if you weren't perpetually late."

"Sorry," I replied, dropping my bag against the wall.

He let out a small chuckle. "Honestly, I kind of like it. It's comforting how you're always so you." He then looked me up and down. "You look great, by the way. I like the outfit."

"Thanks," I replied, my cheeks warming a bit. I could sense that there was more behind his words, especially as his eyes lingered along my body.

"Let's get started," he said, unlocking his phone. "I pulled up your latest physical test stats and made a list of things to work on."

"What?" I asked, a bit taken aback. But then, this was very Luke. He was always about the facts and stats, very much unlike me.

"It looks like you did two push-ups, and the pack requires a minimum of twenty for women, so that's something we'll definitely have to work on. And your half-mile run time is also far below what's required. After today, dress warm, because we're going jogging. On the bright side, your sit-ups and sprints are to standard." He gave me a quick smile and put his phone back in his pocket. "We can start out with some stretching."

I walked with him to the mats and followed his lead. I'd imagined it would be more intimate than it was in reality. Luke was straight to business, never mind that I was his mate and dressed in a really low-cut sports bra. Afterward, we moved over to the free weights area, and Luke handed me a couple of dumbbells.

"I have to lift these?" I whined, giving him a pout.

He gave my arm a squeeze. "I'm going easy on you today. These are only fifteen pounds each. Come on, you're a werewolf."

"Rawr," I said flatly.

"Let's start with some bent-over rows." He grabbed a pair of weights for himself, which I noted were significantly larger than mine, and demonstrated.

"Nice ass," I said, winking.

"Flirting isn't going to get you out of this. Now, come on."

"Hmm, it usually works," I replied, getting into position.

"Sounds like I need to start auditing the sparring sessions if the trainers are going easy on cute civilians."

"At least you still think I'm cute."

He put his hand gently on my lower back. "Lucy, of course I think you're cute. You're probably the hottest girl I've ever met. I've always thought that."

"Then why'd you stop fucking me?" I asked, and it came out with more of a bite than I meant for it to.

He let out a sigh and let the question hang in the silence. I straightened my back and stared at him, wondering if he'd take it as a rhetorical question or if he'd actually answer.

Surprisingly, after a few moments, he did. "Because it was a lot for me. Everything. Becoming a father before I'd planned to, having to lead as a beta, Libby being colicky, everything you were going through. And then . . ." His voice trailed. He shook his head, as if there was something he'd reconsidered telling me. "It was just a lot."

"You wished I was Jasmine, right?" I asked, with that same aggression, too emotional to reel in my attitude.

"What?" He widened his eyes.

"Admit it."

He let out another sigh.

"Goddess, why can't you just be honest with me, Luke?"

"Okay, is that what we're doing? Being honest?"

"For once, can we be?" My voice broke slightly. Did I want to hear it if he *did* still have a thing for my ex-friend?

"Okay, let's sit." He took the weights from me and placed them on the ground next to a bench, then pulled me down to sit next to him.

"So . . ." I started.

He blinked a few times and then opened his mouth. "Look, I care about Jasmine."

"I fucking knew it!" I shouted, seeing red. Ready to go kick everything within my vicinity.

"Calm down, Lucy. I didn't finish what I was saying, okay?"

I rolled my eyes, wondering how much further he was going to drive the dagger into my heart.

"I care about her the way I care about my family. I still feel guilty about everything I put her through. And the thing is, even after we rejected each other, I just can't push away this innate compulsion I have to protect her. But she gave me an ultimatum. And when it came down to it, I wasn't in love with her. Even with how much the mate bond pulled us together and all those things it made me feel. Even with trying to force myself to love her. At the end of the day, I was in love with you. I chose you, Lucy. And that should count for something."

Something inside me burned, my blood steaming. "You feel guilty for how much you hurt her. But do you even feel anything about how much you've put me through? I've always been 100 percent devoted to you. There was never any doubt in my mind that we should be together. But you're always pushing me away." A tear slid down my cheek as all the times he asked me for space played out in my mind.

"I know I'm not perfect, and I haven't been the best mate to you. But, Goddess be damned, I've tried, Lucy," he said with passion, raising his voice.

"Have you though? Or have you just blamed me for everything that's wrong between us?" I glared at him.

He took a deep breath and replied, "To be fair, Lucy, you haven't exactly made it easy. Even ignoring everything that went down before you moved out, it's been less than a month since you went in front of the entire pack and told them you were screwing all these different men on me. Do you know how embarrassing that is? Especially when I'm supposed to be leading the pack. I've been reduced to some tabloid headline."

"So, where do we go from here?" I asked. "Is this it? Are you going to ask me for a divorce?"

"That's not what I want. I want us to work things out. I want you to be my mate again and eventually move back into the pack-house." He took several steady breaths and softly said, "I miss you, Lucy."

I could sense all of Luke's sentiments as he said that and knew it was genuine. There was a lot of pain behind his words. He was clearly just as affected by our dysfunctional relationship as I was. When his emotions came over me like that and flowed through me, I had a hard time focusing. The mate bond could be so distracting and make me so easily forget why I was upset in the first place.

"I'm trying, Luke," I said. "That's why I'm training now, trying to be a better mom, and helping Jasmine and Tyler with their social committee. I admit I wasn't always the best mate." I paused and cringed, the admission feeling unnatural. But I pushed through it and continued, "Especially as a beta mate. But I'm working on that now, okay?"

"I really appreciate it." He brought his hands to my upper arms and moved closer to me, placing his forehead to mine. "I really do."

Our noses touched. We were the closest physically that we had been in months. I didn't know if I'd ever be this close to Luke again. It was so strange. There was a time when we'd always been this close, when this had been natural. And now, it was as if we were strangers who didn't quite know how to connect anymore. Touching my skin to his was almost foreign.

He moved away and broke whatever was going on between us at that moment. "Let's get back to work. You said you want to train, right?"

"Right," I replied, letting out a quiet sigh, a plea for things to go back to how they once were.

Chapter 10

The list I'd put together was taped to my mirror—a reminder for each morning so I could set my intentions. It was a Monday, the day that Jasmine and Tyler met for their Social Development Committee meeting. After being so let down during the last meeting, I'd spent a lot of time thinking up other ideas.

I went through my workday as normal, although a part of me couldn't reel in the thoughts that kept spiraling out of control. I was trying to get to a better place, but Luke kept pushing his way back to the forefront of my mind.

There was a time when he had been a welcome distraction. But now, with our relationship on such shaky ground, it forced me to address and reflect on everything that was off-kilter. Something I hated to do. Why couldn't life just be perfect all the time? Why did there constantly have to be problems?

"You're overkneading." Valerie brought me back to reality. "I think it's time to move on to the muffins."

I let out a sigh.

"If you're going through a crisis, you can just tell me you know."

"I'm not going through a crisis."

"I can give you the crisis hotline just in case."

"What?"

"Maybe you don't want to talk to me, but you'd be willing to talk to someone anonymously."

Then something clicked in my head. "Valerie, you're a genius!" I exclaimed.

"I wasn't expecting that reaction, but I can get that phone number for you. And you know, you can also talk to me anyt—"

"No, I don't need the number. But thanks for the idea!" I said, pulling out the muffin tins.

"You're welcome?" Valerie tilted her head at me and walked away.

After work, I made my way over to the packhouse. Jasmine and Tyler were exactly where I expected to find them on the third floor, in Jasmine's office.

Right before I entered, I stopped, realizing they were deep in a private conversation. I probably shouldn't have, but I couldn't help myself. I loved listening in on things people didn't want me to know.

"Can't you adopt?" Jasmine asked.

"We've looked into it, but most werewolf adoptions are done through pack temples, and it's hard to find one that will adopt out to us," Tyler replied, sounding defeated.

"Oh, wow, I didn't know," Jasmine said in a soothing voice. "Goddess, there are all these things I just never thought about. I guess something else to add to our list of changes to work on."

He sighed. "Yeah. With Jack becoming gamma, he's just been thinking about, if the title continues in the pack, how nice it would be to see our pup succeed him."

He had? I had no idea. I had always just assumed Jack didn't want pups. But why had I assumed that? And why had Jack never told me? That now-too-familiar icky, sour feeling began to form in my stomach and chest again. Jasmine, who'd only known her own brother for a couple years, was far closer to him than I'd ever been to any of mine. Here he was revealing his private woes to her, something Jack had never done with me. Even when Jack came out to the family, I was one of the last to know.

"Wow, yeah, I totally get that," Jasmine replied.

"We might try to find a surrogate. I guess we have time."

"Oh, yeah, that's a good idea. Maybe you could find someone."

"It's just tough because I'm not sure that there's such a thing as a werewolf surrogacy service. We'd probably have to cut a deal with someone." Tyler chuckled. "Meet some woman in a back alleyway. We'll hand her a wad of cash and a jar of Jack's baby batter."

Jasmine laughed at Tyler's joke, and I decided that that was a good moment for me to enter. "I'm here for the meeting," I greeted the two of them.

"Hi, Lucy," Jasmine said, and she couldn't sound less excited to see me.

"Hi!" I replied brightly, not allowing her to know she got to me, walking straight toward the chair she had in the corner by her bookshelf. I dragged it over to her desk so I could sit with the two of them before making myself comfortable. "So what's on the agenda for the meeting today?"

"The uzhe," Tyler replied, shuffling some papers. "Are you now an official member of our committee?"

"Duh!" I replied. "And I have an awesome idea!"

"Okay, let's hear it." Tyler leaned back in his chair.

"We need a pack crisis hotline. An anonymous one. Where people can call in. And it can be either because they're having a hard time and need someone to talk to or because they're having problems around the pack that they're too scared to report. Like with discrimination or something."

At first, no one said anything, and I slumped my shoulders, thinking they wouldn't like my idea again. But then Tyler straightened up and broke the silence. "Wait, that's actually a good idea!"

Jasmine blinked a few times. "I can't believe we didn't think of it ourselves. That would be perfect. One of my initiatives has been to reduce sexual harassment with the warriors. And if they had a way to report it anonymously, that could actually help a lot with figuring out who the culprits are so we can investigate."

"And it could give the queer pack members someone to talk to who could provide them with resources to help them out of bad situations." Tyler nodded along.

"I wonder what we'd have to do to get one set up." Jasmine flipped open a notebook. "What are some things we'd have to think of?"

"We'd have to get volunteers to take the calls. And we'd need to decide whether we want to leave it open just certain hours or twenty-four hours a day."

"I guess we'd have to see how many volunteers we're able to get," Jasmine replied.

"I'll volunteer!" I offered. This was brilliant. I could finally be involved in pack leadership. And it was something that didn't require physical training. It was essentially talking on the phone, which I was great at.

"Lucy, you do realize that you'd have to keep your mouth zipped. You'd be having very sensitive discussions with pack members—things they're not even telling their families." Jasmine gave me a penetrating stare.

"Of course I understand!" I scoffed. "Think about it. I knew my brother was gay for years and I never told anyone! Not even you, even though you were my best friend." Take that!

"Once we get it set up, we'd get you training, and we could see where it goes," Tyler said. "But Jasmine is right. This would be a very serious job. Pack members' lives could be on the line."

I crossed my arms and sat back in my chair, feeling attacked. It was clear as day that neither of them were confident in me. But I wasn't one to back down from a fight. "Look! I can do this! Whatever you thought of me before, just forget about it. This is the new Lucy. I'm going to be the best beta mate this pack has ever had. And you can trust me to do this!"

Jasmine let out a deep breath. "Okay, Lucy."

"We'll give you a shot," Tyler said.

"I won't let you down!" I said, standing up. "I'll even research all the logistics to get it set up, and I'll have a report for you at the next meeting."

As I walked out the door, I smiled to myself. I finally felt like things were starting to click into place, and I was making some real, positive changes. Then I remembered something and doubled back. I peeked my head into the doorway. "And, Jasmine!"

She sat up, turning to look at me.

"You and Blake need to pick a date night because I'm going to watch Ryker and Aria on a day of your choosing."

"You don't have to do th—"

"I'm doing it. So pick a day. And I'll bug you until you do," I said and then left before she could protest.

Chapter 11

I arrived early on the evening I was set to babysit Ryker and Aria. It was also Luke's night with Libby, so I offered to watch all three. I figured Aria and Ryker were still infants, so how hard could it really be? Especially since they weren't colicky like Libby had been. I'd just put them to bed and deal with Libby the rest of the evening.

I pushed the door open to find Luke sitting at the dining room table with some paperwork. He lifted his head, and his light brown eyes instantly locked with mine. "Hey," he said.

"Hey," I replied. "I'll go let Eleanor know I'm here, so she can go home."

He smiled. "Actually, Eleanor already went home. Blake and Jasmine took their pups early, and I didn't want her to stay just for Libby."

"Where's Libby?" I asked, looking around.

"Napping for once." He chuckled. "She's on the couch. But I wouldn't disturb her unless you want a battle to break out in the packhouse."

"You think I don't know that?" I put my hand on my hip, annoyed that Luke thought I didn't know my own daughter and the dangers of waking her from a nap.

He stood up and walked over, stepping directly in front of me. "I didn't mean anything by that. Sorry."

I breathed in his scent. No matter how much he hurt and aggravated me, I couldn't hate his smell. It always snaked its way into me and forced me to inhale like a thirsty woman who'd been crawling through the desert with no water for several days. I forced myself to concentrate and not allow it to derail my train of thought.

I shook my head and said, "How am I supposed to take it when you're always attacking me as a mother?" He opened his mouth, but a surge of emotion came over me, and I spoke before he could. "It's not like you're any better as a father. You only get away with it because you're a male. You're allowed to devote your life to your job and expect either the mother or grandmothers to watch your pup. You're allowed to just clap your hands together and say you're too busy being the provider. But you know what, Luke, you're just as responsible for Libby as me. And if you expect me to be the main caretaker, you could at least be a good mate to me. And you haven't even done that."

"That's not fair." He narrowed his eyes at me. "I think I've been more than patient with you. I've given you everything you wanted. I've completely supported you ever since we found out you were pregnant. You didn't have to work and were able to leave when you were going through your depression. And you haven't even had to do anything. You had a nanny during the day, we have cooks and cleaners in the packhouse. All I ever asked of you was to be a respectable beta mate. To act appropriately in front of the pack. And you couldn't even manage that. You still can't manage that."

"No, you're wrong, Luke!" I exclaimed.

"How am I wrong?" He crossed his arms, taking a defensive stance.

"You have not given me everything I've wanted."

"Are you kidding me?"

"I think it's funny you think you have!"

"What the fuck have you wanted that I haven't given you?" He raised his voice. Luke was usually pretty good at keeping his cool, but it was clear he was on shaky ground.

"I needed a fucking mate! I needed someone to be there for me as my mate. You may have checked off some stupid checklist, so you can act like you did everything right. But you weren't really there for me the way a mate should be. When I'd try to talk to you about how I was hurting, you'd act like I was just bitching. And when I'd need you to hold me, you'd pull away. The more I begged for your love and affection, the more hours you'd work. I don't need someone who just throws money at a problem! I need a fucking mate, Luke!"

He opened his mouth, but I didn't want to hear his lame excuses anymore, so I said what I knew he was going to anyway. The same thing he always did. "I know I made some mistakes and did some stuff that you didn't like." And that feeling came back, that uncomfortable feeling where I had to admit he was at least partially right. My mistakes flashed before my eyes—the excessive drinking, flashing the nightclub, constantly pawning Libby off on my mom, and announcing to the whole pack I was sleeping around. It took everything in me not to either throw up or pass out from having to acknowledge that these things did, indeed, occur. I pushed through it and continued, "But I'm owning up to it now, and I'm making an effort to be better. What exactly are you doing?"

He was about to speak again, but I interrupted him before he could get a word out, "Where's Ryker and Aria? I'm here to work. So just tell me where they are and you can go do your important beta shit."

He sighed, shaking his head, and said, "Upstairs on the alpha floor with Blake and Jasmine."

"Thanks," I replied and turned on my heel to head upstairs.

I took two steps at a time, annoyed by my conversation with Luke. No matter what, he only ever saw how he was hurt, what I'd done to him. But he didn't see how much he'd hurt me, or I realized, why I'd done some of the more egregious things in his mind. He'd unwittingly pushed me to act out. He'd turned a totally sane woman crazed—crazed with desperation for the person she'd promised herself to, begging him to love her back the way she needed.

Voices echoed down the hallway from the common bathroom as I stepped off the stairs onto the alpha floor. The door was wide open, with light streaming out onto the carpet, so I figured it was safe to approach.

As I stopped in the doorway, I was about to announce my presence when I stopped. My breath shuddered, and my ribs squeezed my insides so tight I thought I might choke. I quietly observed the scene in front of me. Blake and Jasmine were bathing their pups in the bathtub, which should have registered as completely normal and nothing to cry over. But it was just the way they were with each other—their chemistry. All I could see was deep love and connection.

Blake chuckled in a way I'd never seen him chuckle, his whole face lit up as Jasmine splashed their babies. He inched closer to her, rubbing her back gently, and she glanced up at him, a huge smile on her face. The two of them were lost in their own world, completely oblivious to me gawking at them.

Had Luke and I ever been like that? Or had I always bulldozed him into being with me? A heaviness settled in my stomach, a regret for forcing something that was probably never truly meant to be. I had never questioned it before—the relationship between

Luke and me seemed so natural for so many years. But now, watching the way Jasmine and Blake looked at each other, I began to reflect back on all my prior actions. Even when I'd first approached him, he hadn't seemed that interested. But I fought against his hesitations and did everything I had to in order to capture him like a fish in the ocean.

What work had he ever done to either get me or keep me? He'd always had one foot out the door. Never really agreeing to commit, but more than happy to welcome me into his bed on a monthly basis when I'd go visit him in Canada during the couple years he was on mission. On my eighteenth birthday, he was more than ready to break up after we found out we weren't mates. Even though we'd had two years of history, two years when I'd given my heart to him completely without asking much in return, he still couldn't agree to be my chosen mate without knowing what his other option was.

And, I wondered, had he had a hunch that it was Jasmine even then? At the time, I hadn't thought much about it, but he did constantly ask me how she was doing and seemed to listen extra attentively when I'd tell him stories that included her. He was a bit protective as well. Like when I'd tell him a story about her being teased by someone at school, it would be as if he were ready to go back to the pack and take care of the asshole himself. I'd push it away, never believing that the love of my life would even consider doing something as hurtful as being with my best friend.

My eyes burned, and tears threatened to fall as I blinked rapidly to keep them at bay.

"Lucy?" Jasmine said my name. She tilted her head at me, probably wondering why I was staring at her and her family like a creep.

I sniffed and forced myself to straighten up and act normal. "I'm here. So I can take over now. You guys are free to go on your date."

"Are you okay?" Jasmine stood up, balancing her hand on Blake's shoulder, a pitying expression on her face. I noted Blake instantly adjusted his arms and body so he'd be able to catch her in case she fell, unlikely considering how well-trained Jasmine was. But it was as if his every impulse was to protect her and keep her safe.

"Yeah, perfect," I replied. "Why wouldn't I be?"

"Uh, okay," she replied, clearly not believing me. "Let me get the pups dried and dressed, and I'll come downstairs once they're ready."

"Okay," I replied and spun around to head back to the main floor, hoping Luke wouldn't be there. I could sense he was still inside the packhouse, within my vicinity, but hopefully he'd gone into his office or something. I didn't want to talk to him again for the remainder of the night. Probably a big ask considering I'd be watching all the pups *in* the packhouse.

I was about to go check on Libby when I heard heavy steps following behind me.

"Lucy," Blake called out, and I turned around to face him. He approached me, and I instantly knew this was not going to be a fun conversation. His shoulders and jaw were both stiff, and he penetrated me with an intense gaze, his eyes starting to take on the evil look they sometimes did when he was pissed off. Goddess, what did I do now?

"Yes?" I asked, holding my chin up, not letting him know he intimidated me.

"I'm putting a lot of trust in you tonight. Frankly, trust that you haven't earned." He paused, not breaking eye contact with me, his sharp blue eyes piercing me and chilling my bones.

I impulsively gulped.

In a menacing voice, he continued, "I would die, torture, and kill for those pups. And if anything happens to them, I will not show mercy. I've made that mistake before. Never again." He then turned and walked back upstairs.

"Mama!" Libby wobbled over to me with Luke trailing behind, her favorite stuffed wolf in hand.

I bent down to hug her, comforted, especially after being threatened by Blake. Sometimes it seemed like Blake's favorite activity was intimidating me. Like he got some sick pleasure from it.

"I have to run some patrols tonight," Luke said. "You'll be okay with all three pups by yourself?"

"Why wouldn't I be?" I asked with a bite. "Plenty of people have three or more kids and they're fine. You and Blake could have some more confidence in me."

"Okay, I was just going to offer to invite my mom over, just in case."

"Luke, I'm fine. The whole point is that I'm being helpful. And it's not helpful if your mom has to give up her evening to help me. That defeats the whole purpose."

He nodded. "Okay. I appreciate it, Luce." He gave me a sweet smile. He began to turn away but then stopped. "It hasn't gone unnoticed that you've been making an effort lately. It means a lot to me, and I hope we'll be able to work things out."

I gave him a half smile, not sure how to respond. While I was grateful that my work had been noticed, I still didn't really feel like Luke heard me during our conversation earlier. It seemed like he believed it was on me to do all the work and he was completely blameless.

"Come on, Libby, let's get you some food before Ryker and Aria come downstairs." I took my daughter's hand and led her into the kitchen to see what Connie had left for dinner. I was pleased to find her homemade spaghetti and meatballs waiting on the stovetop, along with fresh salad and garlic bread. She must have known Libby would be staying overnight because that was one of the foods she was willing to eat.

I made her a small bowl of spaghetti with two meatballs and sat her in the booster seat that she'd recently transitioned to. I wasn't really sure she needed it, which wasn't surprising considering how tall both Luke's and my families were. She was above average height for her age and didn't show any signs of stopping.

Jasmine came into the kitchen just as I was finishing up with Libby. I'd miraculously gotten her to eat most of her food without too much of a fuss. And I'd now handed her a cookie for dessert.

"Hey, Lucy, thanks for watching the pups tonight." She gave me a closed half smile. "I just fed both of them, and Blake is putting them into their cribs now, so they should be okay for a while. Here's the baby monitor." She handed me a white, plastic object with a screen. "There's more milk in the fridge. If you need anything, just call me or Blake. And if you can't get a hold of us, I wrote down the phone numbers for both my parents, my grandparents, Blake's mom, and his grandparents here." She placed a paper down on the counter. "If they get fussy, usually rocking them and playing music helps, and—"

"Jasmine, chill!" I cut her off. "Libby was their age before. I know what I'm doing."

She took a deep breath in and let it out. "Okay."

"Now, go have fun on your date with Blake and let me handle it. They'll be fine. There's nothing to worry about. And I hope you're not wearing your granny panties."

"I don't wear granny panties."

"Just saying. Tease Blake a little. He needs to loosen up."

"I don't need sex advice," she responded. "Blake and I are fine in that department." She crossed her arms in a really unwelcoming way, and I realized I'd overstepped a boundary.

"I was just trying to be friendly. Like friends are with each other," I tried to explain, letting out a sigh.

"We're not friends, okay? I appreciate you offering to watch my pups so Blake and I can have a night out, even if I'm not completely convinced it's for selfless reasons, but it doesn't make up for everything you've done that's been selfish and hurtful."

"Okay," I said, not knowing what else there was to say. Defeated, all I could manage was, "Have fun tonight. I'll take care of everything here at the packhouse."

She nodded. I could tell she wasn't convinced at all that I was capable, and it was really bothering me how little faith everyone seemed to have in me. I was a mother for Goddess's sake!

I finally pushed Jasmine and Blake out the door, but not before Blake put his pointer and middle fingers to his eyes and then pointed them at me. I rolled my eyes. "You're not in the Mafia,

Blake. So stop acting like it," I yelled out to him as they got into his car.

He gave me one final glare and then they were gone.

Of course, as soon as their car disappeared down the street, the pups' cries rang out from the baby monitor. I sighed and made my way upstairs with Libby trailing. Ryker and Aria, whose cribs were in the same room, were both in hysterics.

I took them both out, cradling a pup in each arm, something that actually took a lot more skill than I'd imagined. I tried to calm them by taking a seat with both of them in the rocking chair. But no matter how long I rocked them, they wouldn't stop. And soon Libby was getting frustrated and started whining for my attention, pulling at my legs.

The whole evening basically went like that. Every time I thought Ryker and Aria were okay, they needed something. And when I'd try to calm them down by, say, changing their diapers, Libby would become bored and start bothering me again.

When it was finally time to put Libby down for bed, she had a full meltdown. I had just about pulled my hair out by the time she finally fell asleep, and of course, that's when Luke conveniently showed up. I walked past him without saying a word and made my way downstairs, my hand so tight on the baby monitor I was surprised I didn't break it.

I sat down on the living room couch and flipped on the TV, hoping to relax until Blake and Jasmine got back. Luke took a seat next to me, put his elbows on his knees, and ran his hands through his hair. I could sense the anxiety coming from him. I didn't know why he sat down next to me. I gave him every opportunity to leave me alone tonight. Finally, he said, "I hate this."

"You hate what?"

"I hate how things have turned out between us. I hate how every time I try to talk to you, you have an attitude with me. I hate how when I say something, you take it the wrong way."

"Maybe because every time you say something, it's bullshit," I replied.

"Care to elaborate?"

"I've already elaborated several times, and at this point, I can't believe anything except you're deliberately choosing not to listen to me."

He didn't respond but stayed sitting next to me as I flipped through the channels and eventually settled on some dumb dating TV show. Something mindless to zone out to, something to make me feel better about the trainwreck my life had become.

"You'd totally win if you were on one of those shows, no doubt," Luke said.

"Hmm?"

"First of all, you're prettier than all of them. But it's not only that. You have this enchanting and charismatic way about you. When you like someone, you make them feel so valued and special. You're a great listener, and you're the type of person who always has someone's back when it comes down to it. You definitely charmed me when I first met you."

"Something I deeply regret now."

"Don't say that."

I lowered the volume and turned toward him. "I've thought a lot about this, Luke, and I've realized it was always me doing the work. I was the one chasing you and taking the lead in the relationship. Yeah, you're a nice guy and say a lot of sweet things. But you also have no idea what you actually want. You just let other people decide for you. Even now, I think the only reason you're sitting here and saying these things to me is because we marked each other and now you're stuck. Otherwise you would've moved on to some other sucker who's attracted to you for all the wrong reasons."

I could sense that what I said affected him. He didn't reply, but all his ill feelings flowed into me, choking me. And I felt a little bad for him. After all, he had been raised to follow Blake's commands and put the pack ahead of himself. Who could blame him for being so frustratingly spineless?

"I just wish . . ." he started.

"Wish what?"

"That I knew how to fix this."

"You really want to know how?"

"Yeah, tell me."

"I'm owning up to the things I've done wrong now. I'm working on myself. But this wasn't all just me. This is you as well. And until you acknowledge that, it's never going to be fixed."

We sat like that for the rest of the evening, turned toward the TV, like we were just a normal couple on a normal night. But I could feel everything Luke felt, which kept me distracted enough that I couldn't relax like I'd wanted.

"Let me go check on the pups," I said, standing up. But before I could move too far, Luke grabbed my arm.

I turned to look at him. His eyes were full of emotion as he spoke. "Lucy, even if things are bad right now, I want you to know that I still love you. And I want us to be a family again someday."

Something inside me broke a little. I wanted to run into his arms and tell him I love him too. I wanted all of this to end so badly. But I held it together and just said, "Okay."

By the time I made it back down the stairs after checking on everyone, Jasmine and Blake entered the front door. Jasmine's cheeks were flushed and she giggled, standing on her tippy toes and leaning against Blake's body while he kissed her. I cleared my throat and they moved apart, turning to look at me.

"How are the pups?" Jasmine asked.

"They're good. No problems."

"Thanks for watching them. I don't think either of us realized how badly we needed this night out." She gave me a big smile. The sides of Blake's mouth lifted upward slightly, but he didn't really smile. He also didn't scowl at me, so I guess that meant he was happy. She skipped past me up the stairs.

"Are you good to get home?" Blake asked. "You don't need a ride or anything?"

"I'm not far. Still living in the apartments," I replied.

"Okay." He nodded and similarly headed upstairs.

I threw on my winter coat and boots and stepped outside into the chilly air. It was nice on nights like this. The atmosphere was crisp and quiet, the stars above us clear and bright, and it felt like the world was still. I breathed in the cool air, inhaling the smell of winter. My boots crunched against a fresh dusting of snow as I walked home.

When I finally made it back to my apartment, I blew out a sigh of relief and decided to pour myself a glass of wine. It was definitely not a fun night, but I felt oddly proud of myself for getting through it. And it was actually quite nice how Jasmine seemed genuinely thankful before I left.

I still couldn't understand why she continued to call me selfish. As if she wouldn't have done the same had the situation been reversed. I mean, she must have understood now with how much she loved Blake, no? Couldn't she see how hurt she would be if I came along and blindsided her by dating him?

As soon as I settled on the couch and took my first few sips, Madison came strutting in, a huge smile on her face, not much different than Jasmine's. Was everyone having a good night except me? I took another sip, trying to drown out my self-loathing.

"Ahh! Cole is so amazing!" Madison plopped herself down on the couch next to me. "He's so wise and intelligent. I could just spend hours listening to him lecture me about Artemis's scriptures. And when he guides me through religious meditation, it's an experience on a whole other level! He's just teaching me so much!"

"Sounds like he's also teaching you how to finally get in touch with what's between your legs!" I snickered.

Madison scoffed. "It's not like that! I'm obviously saving myself for my mate. And you wouldn't understand. You can't see men past what's between their legs."

"What's that supposed to mean?"

"All you ever said about Luke when you talked about him was how good he was in bed. I'm pretty sure I know every position you ever did it in, and we're all privy to the fact that he luuurves when you swallow." She put two fingers in her mouth and made a gagging noise. "I think it's way better when you connect with someone on an intellectual and spiritual level."

"How would you know if you've never even had sex? What if the guy is terrible in bed? Erin told me about a guy she was with that would just stick it in, last five seconds, and that was it. What if *Cole* is like that?"

Madison huffed. "Cole isn't like that."

"You say that like you know."

Madison blushed but didn't say anything.

"He is married you know. And he's our fucking priest!"

"It's not like that!" she said, got up, and walked to her room, shutting the door behind her.

Chapter 12

Luke continued to train me on a semiweekly basis, and we seemed to have mutually decided not to bring up everything that we were internally seething about again. Maybe it was for the better. At least this way we were amicable with each other and not failing spectacularly at communicating.

"I'm impressed," Luke said at one point in the middle of my sit-ups, finally breaking our mutual silence on the subject. "You haven't been slacking at all with your training. You've been showing up, and you've actually been working really hard. I've seen a lot of improvement."

"You say that like you had no faith in me," I replied.

"I always knew you could do it if you just disciplined yourself. And I only say that because you didn't for a while."

"Are you always going to hold that against me?"

He gently touched my knee. "Honestly, Lucy, I'm not mad about it anymore. I've thought a lot about what you said to me, and I think I just have a hard time seeing things from your point of view sometimes because we both think so differently. But I get it now. You weren't in a good place. And while I'm the type of person who just pushes through it and does what I have to and what is expected of me, you're not like that. I pressed you too much when I should have been listening to you instead."

"I'm glad you finally get it."

"I'm going to make more of an effort to try to see things from your perspective from now on."

"Thanks."

"But can you also do me the favor of also trying to understand where I'm coming from? I honestly wasn't coming down on you to be an asshole. It's because it's really important to me to be a good beta to the pack. My dad was incredible at his job, and still is when he jumps in to help, and it's so hard to live up to that. But I try my damn hardest every day."

"Your dad probably wasn't always good at it. He had you when he was older, so you have no idea what he was like in his twenties. Same with your mom. Yeah, now she's like the pinnacle of a beta mate. But she was young once too. I hate that I'm constantly pitted against someone who's almost forty years older than me."

"You know, my mom does stick up for you. She always liked you."

"Yeah, except when she found out Jasmine was your mate."

"She eventually got over it." He sighed. "Are you going to hold that against me for the rest of our lives? I didn't choose Jasmine to be my mate, and my parents are very traditional, so they were obviously going to want me to be with her. Also, I think you forget that Jasmine's crazy alpha family literally came to our pack before and threatened us over a mate bond."

I didn't reply. This was another one of those conversations we'd beaten to death. I didn't think I could ever make Luke understand how devastating it was for me when it happened. I'd loved him fully for four years, we'd been moving toward becoming chosen mates, and it would have hurt no matter who ended up being his fated mate. But the fact that it was my *best friend*? How does someone just move past that?

"Okay, let's go do some sparring outside," Luke said when it was clear the conversation wasn't going to continue. He jumped up and put out his hand. I took it and he helped me to my feet with barely any effort. His hand lingered a little on mine, and then he slowly withdrew. "Sorry, I just missed feeling the sparks. It's such a nice feeling."

I couldn't disagree with him. It had been so long since I'd snuggled up against him, the sensation running all along my skin, simultaneously arousing and soothing me. The few moments our hands touched were barely adequate, and it made me realize how starved I was to have him back. But I wasn't ready to just forgive him.

I followed him outside to the field. It was well into the evening, and the winter darkness had already set in hours ago. It was just the two of us, a fresh dusting of snow covering the field, fallen since whenever it had last been cleaned. The only light was the bit of illumination streaming from the windows of the gym a few yards away and the glow from our night vision.

"Wolf form today?" Luke asked.

"Yeah, sure," I replied. I was about to go to the partition to strip down, but there was no one on the field except the two of us, and it wasn't like Luke hadn't seen my body a million times already. I began to peel off the bit of gym clothes I had on and paused just as I was about to unsnap my bra. At first, I couldn't tell if it was me or him . . . No, it was definitely him—he was turned on. I peeked over my shoulder, instantly catching his eyes on me.

He immediately turned his gaze downward, his cheeks reddening. He grabbed the bottom hem of his T-shirt and pulled it over his head, revealing his well-sculpted warrior torso to me—the one I used to spend hours tracing my fingers along, not leaving a single muscled crevice untouched.

I quickly turned away, removed the rest of my clothes, and shifted into my wolf form. But my emotions just became amplified in this form. As wolves, we always turned more feral, relying more on instinct than logic. And my wolf had come to love Luke's now that we'd marked each other. It had been months since we'd really touched each other as mates, and I couldn't stop myself as I sprinted over to him, rubbing my wolf body against his, my fur brushing against him, my snout nuzzling against his neck.

I sensed a warmth that spread from his heart to his limbs, and the calming effect this gesture had on him. His whole demeanor became relaxed. He groomed me with his tongue, licking just along the side of my ear. I purred in response, and my eyes drooped closed. It had been so long since we'd been affectionate like this with each other.

I didn't want to move away. I missed him. I missed this. I missed how it had once been, when this was all we had between us, before all the bitterness and resentment settled into the cracks of our relationship and pried us apart.

After some time, he finally mindlinked me, *"Okay, why don't we begin? I'll start by attacking, and you try to block my attempts."*

I let out a sigh and moved into position as Luke got into his warrior stance. He went easy on me of course—I could tell. But I succeeded in recalling all the blocks for each of his attempts. I imagined that he probably wouldn't have gone easy on Jasmine. He would have probably even tried to trick her to keep her on her toes. In fact, she'd likely put up a good fight with him. And I started to understand more why maybe I wasn't the best match for him. I mean, there's no way he wasn't bored by having to train me. It was the exact reason Kyle had pawned me off on our little brothers.

Because this would have been a chore. At least Luke trained the elementary schoolers, so this wasn't too much outside his normal function.

"*You're doing great, Luce,*" he mindlinked me and gave me an encouraging tilt of his head. And he did seem genuinely pleased when he said that. But I still wondered if he felt like he was missing out, not having a mate who was challenging to spar with.

When we finally finished, I transformed back into my human form and quickly dressed, the cold wind stinging against my bare skin. As I walked back toward the gym, Luke came up beside me, taking my hand in his. My breath caught, and for the first time in so long, I finally felt like maybe we could find our way back to each other again.

"Thanks for training me," I said. "I know you have to take time out of your day to do it. So, thanks."

"I've enjoyed this. It's been nice. I should have offered a long time ago. I don't know why I didn't."

"It's okay. I get it. You were busy. And it's not like I'm a priority, especially for training."

"You are a priority. You're the beta mate." He stopped and took my chin in his hand. "And I'm sorry that I didn't make you feel that way."

I snuggled into his hand. Goddess, I missed this so much. He used to always be like this. When did it stop?

"Kiss me, Luke," I said, my voice raspy with yearning.

He smiled and pecked his lips against mine, and soon, it was like nothing had ever gone wrong between us. He held me tightly, his body warmth making me forget how cold the night was. Our lips twined and my cheeks flushed. I brought my hands to his face, which was just as warm and rough with late evening stubble. I inhaled his musky, sweet scent.

"I miss you, Lucy," he muttered against my lips between kisses.

I abruptly broke contact. "Then I guess you should have never thrown me out like I was a piece of trash." And I turned before sprinting away. I wasn't going to be that easy to get back. This time he could work for it.

The next day, Jack and Tyler insisted Libby and I come over for dinner. They'd been doing this on a monthly basis since I got kicked out of the packhouse. I think it was a wellness check. Considering he'd barely ever lifted a finger when he lived with our family, Jack was actually a pretty good cook. So I didn't mind going, even if they saw me as a charity case.

When I arrived, they both pulled Libby and me in for hugs.

"How's my favorite little hellion niece?" Tyler asked as he wrapped his arms around Libby.

"Hi!" she responded.

"Still being a pain in your mom's butt?"

"Yes." Libby giggled.

"At least she's honest," I said.

"She's just overly persistent like her mom. Won't rest until she gets her way," Jack teased.

"Hey! I'm not that bad!" I defended myself.

"I think there are a few stories that say otherwise." Tyler snickered. "Anyway, come on, let's go eat."

They led me into the kitchen where a plate was ready with dino nuggets for Libby. For the rest of us, they had laid out barbecue chicken thighs, steamed broccoli, and rice pilaf. After working most of the day, I was starving, so I took more than usual when they passed everything around.

Before starting on his own food, Jack gave his niece's shoulder a squeeze. "How are those dino nugs, Lib?"

"Yummy!" she responded, holding one up to show him.

"They look yummy." He smiled at her. "Dino-licious."

She made a laughing noise while she had a mouth full of food, which caused some of it to dribble down her chin.

"Ptery-ble table manners, Lib." Jack smiled, grabbing a napkin to wipe at her mouth.

"Are you guys trying to adopt?" I blurted out.

"What?" Jack froze in place, his shoulders stiffening.

"Like did you want to have a pup?" I clarified.

"We're fine with the way things are," Jack responded almost immediately.

Everyone went back to eating, but Jack's response didn't sit comfortably with me. He clearly didn't trust me. I slumped my shoulders, my throat starting to get a bit scratchy. My own brother didn't want to share his struggles with me and was shutting me out. And this only stung so much more after I'd witnessed Tyler being so open with his own sister. Why couldn't Jack and I have that kind of relationship? Had I done something wrong?

That sickly, sour feeling resurfaced. I'd clearly not made myself the type of person Jack could confide in. I didn't want that to be the case anymore. I wanted to fix what I'd done wrong so Jack could trust me and come to me when he needed support. I wasn't just going to let this go. I turned to my brother-in-law. "Tyler, I overheard you talking to Jasmine about wanting a pup."

"You heard that conversation?" he asked, rubbing the back of his neck.

"Is it true? Are you thinking about finding a surrogate?"

Jack fidgeted with his silverware, pushing food around on his plate.

"We haven't decided on anything yet," Tyler replied. "We were just brainstorming. And that was a private conversation."

"Well, I have an idea," I said.

"It's okay, Lucy. We're fine," Jack snapped. Then he softened his voice and said, "How are things going with you, Luce? Tyler tells me you've been helping out with the Social Development Committee."

I sighed. "Listen, about the surrogate thing, I have a really good idea."

The two of them turned toward each other, locking eyes, and I couldn't read what was silently being said. Maybe Jack was even mindlinking Tyler. Unfortunately, neither Tyler nor I had the ability to link back in our human forms even if our mates could, unlike Jasmine who did get that gift by becoming luna.

Finally, Tyler sighed and said, "Okay, Lucy, what's your idea?"

I straightened up. "Well, I'm Jack's sister, right? That means we share a lot of the same genes. So, in theory, if I were your surrogate, it would almost be like your pup was both of yours, right?"

Their mouths dropped. And they glanced back and forth between me and each other. No one said anything for what seemed like forever. I had to hold back from pushing the subject more and instead turned my attention to my food, feeling a bit awkward. Finally, Jack broke the silence. "Lucy, think about what you're offering."

"I have thought about it. And I want to do this. So let me."

"You don't always think things through, Luce. You get an idea and you become impulsive. This is a huge deal."

"Jack!" I replied, impassioned, "I'm your sister. We're family. I'm not just offering this to some rando on the street. Family does stuff like this for each other. It's like what Tyler said to me. What makes a good mom? It's someone who always gives to their pups unconditionally. But that's not just moms. That's *family*. I know you'd have my back no matter what. No matter how much I annoy you."

"Yes, but you're offering to give us your pup. The pup you're going to carry for six months and will then have to give up custody to us. That's so much more than either of us could ever give back to you."

"I mean, you're a warrior!" I flipped my hair behind my back. "At some point, you might have to either save Libby's or my life. So that's not really true."

Jack sighed, sat back in his seat, and grabbed at his hair. After a moment he closed his eyes, and I wondered what he was thinking. He almost seemed frustrated. But I couldn't understand why. I'd just offered him something that he and Tyler clearly wanted. I'd have thought he'd have been happier about the offer.

"I guess you don't just have an empty cavity for a chest. There is a heart in there somewhere," Tyler quipped.

"Do I look metal to you?" I responded.

"You oil yourself enough during the summer that I thought you might be," Tyler replied. I rolled my eyes, and after a beat, he put his hand on my arm and said, "Honestly, Lucy, that has to be one of the most kindhearted things anyone's ever offered. I just don't even know how to react." He held my gaze, and I noticed he seemed to be tearing up a little. He promptly blinked and looked away.

"You can start with 'thank you.'"

He turned back to me, put his palms together as if in prayer, and touched his index fingers to his lips. With an emotion-filled voice, he said, "Thank you."

"You're welcome. And for the record, I'm insulted you didn't think to ask," I said. "Especially since it would get me out of training for a few months."

Jack seemed to finally come out of his daze. The outer corners of his mouth lifted in a small smile.

"I guess you are good at coming up with ideas sometimes," Tyler said.

"We'll think about it. It's a big decision," Jack added. "We probably won't be ready for a few years anyway." He picked up his water glass to take a sip.

"It's going to take Jack some time to get over the image of his sister turkey basting my high fructose porn syrup into her lady parts."

Jack practically spit his water out. "Hey, there's a pup at the table!"

"She's just getting an early lesson on where babies come from," Tyler responded.

"Baby!" Libby said.

"Granted, this lesson might be a bit advanced and unconventional. Probably all going right over her head anyway."

"Sex!" Libby said, resurrecting the word Tyler had previously taught her.

"Tyler, stop trying to corrupt my daughter!" I exclaimed. Then we all laughed. And a warmth spread through my chest. I'd done something good. Really good.

Chapter 13

Jasmine, Tyler, and I got to work on the call center almost immediately. We decided that, to start, we'd just have it open in the evenings until we could get enough volunteers trained to leave it open for more hours. The three of us agreed to each split the evenings up for the time being.

It wasn't too much of a commitment, since it mostly required just being available to take the call if the phone rang. They assigned me to the nights that Luke had Libby. Jasmine took the evenings that Blake didn't have to run patrols, so that he could be there to tend to their pups if a call happened to come in on her evening, and Tyler took the remainder of the nights.

I volunteered to go around the pack and hang up flyers in different places, such as the temple, the elementary and high school, the library, and the clinic. Tyler sat with me the first time around. We'd found guides online for fielding crisis calls, and Tyler went through them with me.

"What is that on your laptop?" I asked, glancing over at his screen where it just looked like a whole bunch of letters and numbers.

"Oh, while looking up a lot of this stuff, I noticed that some centers offer texting and online chatting options. So I'm just sort of playing around, thinking about setting something up for our pack. People might feel more comfortable texting, especially if they still live at home."

"Oh, that's actually a really good idea."

"Yeah, but I also think we need to get some legit counselors to help us. We're kind of just cobbling this together. But we could potentially be getting some people with serious issues that call in."

I reflected on what he said and then an idea came to me. "Oh. Actually, my mom has a friend that works at the hospital at the Autumn Moon Pack. And they have a mental health wing there. Maybe my mom's friend could find someone who's willing to help us out."

"That would be great. Even if they were able to just give us some pointers."

For the first week, we didn't get any calls. I knew we'd just gotten the thing off the ground, but I figured that since we'd never had anything like this before, people would be excited to call in. I mean they had to have had problems with no one to turn to, right? And now they had this!

"It's still new. People don't know if they can trust it yet," Tyler told me one day when I was venting to him.

On my final shift of the second week, I was just about to turn in for the night when a ring on my laptop alerted me that someone was calling in. I fumbled with my headset, throwing it on.

"Hello, this is Lucy at the Midnight Maple Pack Anonymous Hotline. How can I help you?"

"Hi," a girl who sounded young—maybe a young teenager—responded.

"Hi, how can I help you?"

"This line is completely anonymous, right? It's not recorded or anything?"

"No, we don't record our calls. Anything you say will be kept completely confidential unless you want me to tell someone."

"No, please don't tell anyone."

"I promise I won't."

"Okay." She let out a breath. "The thing is, I don't want to go to school anymore. When I wake up, I feel sick, and I tell my parents I can't go. I was able to get away with it for a week. They thought it might be because my wolf is still new. But ever since they took me to the clinic, they don't believe me anymore. But I can't go."

"Why can't you go?"

"It's kind of a long story . . ."

"I'm happy to listen," I replied, trying to encourage her to tell me. I tried to steady my shaking leg from the excitement of getting my first call, and my first opportunity to help.

"Well . . ." she began.

When she didn't continue, I said, "Don't worry. This phone line is totally anonymous. If you have something to get out, this is your chance."

"Okay." The woosh sound of her breathing out a heavy breath sounded in my ear. "The thing is, my brother was always a little weird, but harmless. Then, five years ago, he got his wolf, and he wasn't able to control it. One day, he shifted without warning and attacked me. It left really bad scars on my neck, chest, and stomach. I'm really embarrassed about it, so I try to stay covered up. During training, I always go into the changing room. But one day the girls were just playing around, teasing each other, opening the curtains to the changing rooms of the ones who wouldn't change with everyone else, and they saw it.

"Ever since then, everyone at school makes fun of me. They call my boobs 'scar cha-chas.' And now that spring is coming, and I'm in eighth grade, we're going to start training in our wolf forms. Which means I'm going to probably have to strip down in front of all the other girls who have been making fun of me." She said the last bit in a choked voice, ending the sentence with a sniff.

"Have you told your parents?" I asked.

"No, I can't tell them."

"Why?"

"Because I'm mortified. And plus, I'm afraid they'll get upset. When my brother attacked me, Alpha James banished him. He said he didn't want an uncontrollable wolf in the pack. My parents tried to convince him to let my brother stay, but he wouldn't even listen to them and said it was for the greater good of the pack. Whenever my brother is brought up, they get really depressed, and I don't want to remind them."

"Do you know where your brother is?"

"No. My parents tried to keep track of him for a few years, but we think he eventually just switched over to his wolf form permanently and is just now out there living in the wild as a rogue."

My stomach twisted and my head felt light and staticky. I couldn't imagine going through what this girl was. Even though I was never close to any of my brothers, I'd be devastated if one of them got banished. And my parents would have been wrecks. I began to understand what a big responsibility it was to watch out for every pack member's well-being.

"And Alpha James didn't even consider any other options? Like medication or training?" I asked.

"No. I know everyone in the pack liked him. But I think those people never got on his bad side."

I nodded even though she couldn't see it. I'd heard stories about Blake's dad. Stories that most of the pack was never privy to. "I'm going to help you!" I said. "I can't help you with your brother. But I can definitely help you with the bullies at your school."

"Really?"

"Yeah. So here's the deal. Bullies like it when you react a certain way to their bullying. It makes them feel good to put you down. So what you have to do is not let them see they're hurting you anymore, and they'll get bored. So, for example, when they start calling you names, you should just yawn or roll your eyes or something. Act really bored. You can even say, 'This is getting really boring. You're starting to sound like a broken record saying the same thing to me over and over again.' Practice in the mirror if you have to. Or you could treat them like a little kid. In a baby-talking voice say, 'Do you feel better now that you got all your insecurities out on me? The big scary bully feels big and strong now?'"

She let out a hearty laugh at that.

"If you don't feel comfortable saying that stuff, just find someone you trust to practice with. You can even call here again. I can tell you what evenings I work, and I'll coach you through it."

"You said your name is Lucy?"

"Yes."

"Thanks, Lucy. I'm going to practice that stuff. And you don't mind if I call back?"

"No, not at all. I'd love an update when you get the bullies to finally shut up and leave you alone."

After chatting a bit longer, we finally hung up, and I was pleased with myself. I felt like my first hotline conversation had gone really well. I even texted Tyler to let him know, and he texted me back with several high ten emoji. I went to bed smiling that night, realizing the ceaseless depression I'd been in had finally lifted.

Chapter 14

After my first hotline call, I was riding high. My pride of bringing this idea to the pack and actually making it happen for real radiated from every pore. It gave me the energy to get through the other stuff I struggled with like training with Luke and attending temple services.

I came home Monday evening after stopping by the packhouse to tuck Libby in, so Luke could handle some pack business even though it was a night he had her. The first thing that tipped me off that things weren't right in the world was that Madison's boots, hat, gloves, scarf, and coat were strewn about the floor as I entered our apartment. And then I heard the sniffling. As I turned toward the couch, I found a red, puffy Madison on it, tears streaming down her face, wearing the most hideous flannel muumuu that I'd ever seen, her black hair—which was usually perfectly blown out—flat and matted.

"Goddess, I'm such an idiot, Lucy," she choked out, sobs directly following.

"What happened?" I asked, coming closer.

She wiped at her eyes, taking strangled breaths. Finally, she blubbered out, "I just want to die. I wish Artemis would just kill me. I've made such a huge mistake, and it's not worth living anymore."

"What the hell? Did you kill someone?" I questioned.

"No, that would have been better than what I actually did." She let out a loud wail, wrapping her arms around herself in a comforting gesture.

"Goddess, what could you possibly have done that could be that bad? Did you forget to organize the fridge when you put your groceries inside or something?"

I guess that was the wrong thing to say because her chin trembled and fresh tears poured down her cheeks. Holy Artemis, please tell me she wasn't crying this much over something being messy.

"What is it, Madison?" I pressed. "What happened? I can't help you if I don't know. I mean, if we have to burn a body or torture someone, I need to prepare. I think I can get into Blake's torture chamber. If not, he keeps a knife in his desk."

"Lucy." She looked up at me with the most devastated look I'd ever seen. Her stare was empty and defeated.

"Holy Artemis, Madison," I said, wrapping my arms around her. "Tell me what it is. I promise I won't judge. You may piss me the fuck off, but you're still my friend, and I'm your ride or die."

"I'm pregnant, Lucy," she choked out. "You were right. I've been sleeping with Colvin. And I guess we just felt so guilty about the whole thing that we pretended it wasn't happening and didn't use protection." Her confession turned into sobs as she soaked my shoulder. I held her the way my mom did when I told her about my own pregnancy and how Luke wouldn't leave Jasmine to be with the mother of his child.

Madison's sobs turned to hiccups, which turned to sniffles. Finally, she continued, "But I loved him. He made me feel special. He kept telling me how smart and beautiful I was, and how he wished that I was his mate because we were so perfect for each other."

"So did you tell him?" I asked. "Does he know?"

"Yes," she cried out. "Yes, I told him. And do you know what he said to me?"

"What?"

"He told me that I need to get an abortion right away. He offered to drive me to a human clinic and get it taken care of."

"What!" I exclaimed. "The priest of our temple told you to get an abortion?"

"Yes, and I refused. I told him it was against Artemis's teachings. The Moon Goddess wanted me to carry this pup, and I would not kill him or her."

"How did he take it?"

"Oh, it was so horrible, Lucy!" She choked up, her cheeks glistening with wetness once again. "When I absolutely refused, he called me a slut and homewrecker. And he blamed me for tempting him to sin. When I tried to tell him that it takes two to tango, he said everyone would think the same. Because he's a priest, and only someone evil would tempt and hurt a priest." She hugged me tighter and wept, gasping for air loudly.

My nostrils flared and my entire body heated with full-on rage. Every hair follicle and the nail beds on my fingers and toes tingled with the demand to shift. All I could see was red. "That mother-fucker!" I roared.

Madison winced.

"He is going to regret the day he stroked his dick for the first time and thought about using it for anything other than something to piss out of. That asshole is going to pay. He fucked with the wrong bitch. He is going down!" I stood up, thoughts swirling through my head about all the different ways I could avenge my friend.

"But, Lucy, it's all my fault!" Madison pulled her legs against her body, wrapping her arms around them. "I should have stuck to my morals and beliefs. I knew it was wrong to sleep with anyone who isn't my mate. And I still did. And I can't lie." Her cheeks burned. "I may have seduced him. I would dress more sexy than usual when I'd be working at the temple. Only a bad person would try to tempt a priest. I was clearly in a bad place and was desperate for any male attention, including a priest's! What's wrong with me?"

"No!" I shouted, stepping closer to her. "Madison, if there is one thing I know for sure it's that you're not at fucking fault, and don't ever let some backward-ass religion convince you otherwise. Besides the fact that he's a married man, in a position of power as *both* your employer and your fucking priest, he is also not taking responsibility for the fact that he splooged inside you. He has fucking kids. He knows what happens when you do that."

"But—" Madison began to speak, but I cut her off.

"And don't even get me started on how the temple has so much fucking power over our pack that we can't even get contraceptives at the clinic and abortions are banned. And he's trying to force you to get one? Get fucking real, Madison! This guy is a complete piece of shit. I won't rest until I've fucked him over in every way possible."

"But what about his family?"

"Did he think about them when he stuck his dick inside you?" I crossed my arms, staring down at Madison. "They're better off kicking him to the curb."

"But his wife doesn't work. How will the family survive?"

"The pack has programs to help them. I'm sure her old pack does too. Trust me, she's better off knowing the useless man-child she's mated to so she can make her own decision about her future and whether or not she wants to be with a predator."

Madison sniffed. "It just hurts so much."

I sat back down next to her and pulled her against me. "It's going to hurt, maybe for a while. But you'll eventually move on and be happy again. Time heals all wounds." I spoke the words my mom had to me so many times, recalling how comforted I'd always been when she'd hold me like this and tell me everything was going to be all right.

Chapter 15

The next day I went back to work. Before she went to bed, Madison told me she couldn't go back to her job at the temple and would have to figure something else out. I told her not to worry. I was working now and had some extra income from Luke, so I told her I'd help her out if it came down to it, but only if she'd stop harassing me about everything in the apartment that was even slightly off.

"Crisis," Valerie said as I walked past her to put down my stuff and throw on my apron.

"Goddess, it's like you liked it better when I was always late."

"There's a comfort in people acting predictably. This new you is oddly unnerving."

I rolled my eyes. "Well, you'll be gratified to know there is a crisis, but it's not with me."

"Well? Continue," Valerie said, stepping closer to me, crossing her arms and tilting her head.

Anger throbbed at my temple as I recalled how devastated Madison had been. "That new priest we have is a shit bag."

"That doesn't surprise me one bit. You always hear stories about shit bag priests, but nothing ever happens to them because the temple always holds so much power in packs."

"Yeah, well, I'm going to make fucking sure something happens to this rotten grade-D-but-edible taco meat left between the cushions of a couch for a week while everyone was on vacation."

Valerie jerked her head back. "Damn. What did he do?"

I was about to tell her, Valerie being to me like the big, wise sister I never had. But then I hesitated, knowing it wasn't really my secret to tell.

"I can trust you, right?" I asked.

"Of course," Valerie responded. "Lucy, you're practically a daughter to me. I'd never break your trust. Over all these years, have I ever? Anything you need help with, just tell me, hon."

I nodded. I'd just leave out the details, even though I knew Valerie would never say anything to anyone. She hated the rumor mill just as much as I did. "He knocked up my friend and tried to shut her up about it. I'm ready to steal all of Blake's knives and make some good use of them."

Just as I was about to go into detail about how my first cut would be to his dick, the bell above the door chimed, signaling a customer entering. I stepped in front of the register to place the first order of the morning rush.

Once the last few customers finally left, and I was about to start doing some cleaning, Valerie stopped me. "Look, Lucy. I know you want to cut this asshole into pieces. And I don't blame you. I want to do the same. But you have to start thinking like a beta's mate."

"Like a beta's mate? Our alpha tortures all the fucking time. I think it's within my right."

"Yes, but he's the one that makes the rules and decides who gets a torture sentence. You need to be more calculating. Catch him in the act so that he can't deny it and you can show everyone."

"I like the way you think, Val!" I replied, the gears starting to turn.

And I knew exactly what we had to do, but I needed to get Jasmine involved. This motherfucker was going down!

After work, I was relieved to find Madison at home, burritoed in a blanket in front of the TV.

"Heya, how are you feeling?" I asked, taking a seat next to her.

"It hurts so much." Her voice cracked as she said it. "Both my heart and my boobs."

"Yeah, I remember those days. Do you want a hug?"

"Please," she replied, and I wrapped my arms around her cocooned body.

"I feel like I'm holding an overgrown baby right now."

She let out a little chuckle. "I feel like a baby. You actually make a very nice baby mom."

I smiled, a warmth spreading through my chest. "At least someone thinks so."

"You're being a good mom to me right now." She sniffed a few times.

I held her like that for a bit, and it was actually kind of nice. It had been so long since I'd snuggled with someone who wasn't Libby. I think the wolf part of us craved the touch of others.

After some time I said, "Madison, I'd like to ask your permission for something please."

"What is it?" she asked.

"I want to tell Jasmine what happened."

"What! Why?" She pushed away from me.

"Because that dickwad so-called priest deserves to be castrated."

"Lucy." She sighed. "Maybe I should just let it go. I'll just raise my pup on my own and not tell anyone who the father is."

"That's bullshit!" I exclaimed.

"He has a family. And he wants nothing to do with me." Tears slid down her cheeks. "*I'm* the idiot for believing him when he told me he loved me."

"Are you kidding me? You want him to get away with this? Here he is preaching to everyone to follow the scriptures of Artemis while he's secretly lying his way into girls' pants. Who knows if you were even the first? And you know if you don't report him, he'll just fucking keep doing it. So even if you don't do it for yourself, think about all the other victims he's going to have in the future. You know that Alpha James didn't stop at just one mistress. This asshole won't either."

Madison took a few deep breaths. "I'm just so ashamed."

"Don't be. He lied to you. How were you supposed to know? And each time he does it, he's only going to get that much better at it with practice."

She whimpered.

"Let me tell Jasmine. She used to be our close friend. You know she'd never use the information for bad."

"Jasmine is the sweetest person ever. I know she'd never." After a beat, she continued, "Goddess, this is so hard, but I know you're right. You can tell her. I just can't do it myself. Especially not to Jasmine. She's just so sweet and good. I feel like she'll be so disgusted by what I did."

"Jasmine's not that innocent. Did you forget when she hooked up with *my* boyfriend?"

"But that was her fated mate! You really can't hold that grudge against her forever. I know Jasmine would never have done that intentionally to hurt you."

I scoffed.

"I get that it hurts. This hurts too. But maybe, for once, you should think about things from Jasmine's point of view instead of focusing so much on pitying yourself."

I didn't respond. It still hurt, and I just couldn't move past the deceit I still felt to this day.

After speaking with Madison, I made my way to the packhouse. Libby was napping, so I was able to sneak upstairs to the third floor and found Jasmine in her office just as expected. She was sitting at her laptop with a voice that sounded very similar to Gigi's coming out of it, the two of them laughing at something.

"Is that Gigi?" I asked as I entered her office.

She tipped her head to face me, her posture going rigid.

"Jasmine, you have to see the new alpha who just landed in Alaska! He's so fucking hot! And damn, his Russian accent!" Gigi's voice flowed from the speakers. "Sometimes I tease Tyce and tell him all the things I want the new alpha to do to me, and then he angry fucks the shit out of me. Ten out of ten, highly recommend!"

I stepped behind Jasmine to find Gigi's face on the screen. "I didn't realize Tyce was a cuckold."

"Lucy?" Gigi said, and there was something a bit unwelcoming about her look as she narrowed her eyes at me. Goddess, what was with everyone? I did one thing wrong, and they held it against me forever.

"Lucy, what are you doing here?" Jasmine asked. "Our Social Development Committee meetings are on Mondays."

"Oooh, social committee?" Gigi asked. "I hope you're planning Paige's and my double bachelorette party at these socials! I need one last crazy night out before I become a wifey!"

Jasmine was about to reply when I cut her off. "If anyone should be planning a bachelorette party, it should be me!" I asserted. "Don't worry, I've got it all handled. Jasmine will tell me when it's happening and I'm going to make it perfect. You are going to have the best night of your single life!"

"Lucy, why are you butting in?" Jasmine asked.

I'd noticed she'd become a lot more confrontational in the past year. Especially toward me. After trying to push her for years to not let people walk all over her, she chose me to let this side of her out on.

"C'mon, Jasmine, you know Gigi is going to want a crazy party. Right, Gigi?" I turned to look at Jasmine's screen. "And you know you're not going to know what to do. So let me take care of it!"

Jasmine let out a breath. "We'll talk about this later." She then turned back to her computer. "Gigi, let me call you back."

"'Kay! Tyson's got alpha duty stuff all day, so I'll be around."

Jasmine closed her laptop and sat back in her chair, crossing her arms. "Why are you here? And why are you interrupting my private conversations?"

"Nice to see you too," I replied, taking a seat in the chair in front of her desk and crossing my legs. "And for your information, I actually have a good reason for being here."

"Which is?" she asked in an impatient tone.

"Goddess, you could be a little less snarky toward me. I am the beta mate, and we should at least learn how to work together."

"Lucy, I'm really busy."

"Yeah, I can see that. Talking to Gigi about hot Russian alphas is clearly very important."

"He's Ukrainian, for your information."

"What's the difference?"

"Are you kidding me? There's a literal *war* between the two countries going on right now."

I huffed, my jaw stiff from grinding my teeth so hard, frustrated with the way Jasmine was speaking to me and how she refused to take me seriously.

"Can you please just listen to me?" I raised my voice in annoyance. "This is a serious problem in the pack we need to deal with, and I need your help."

"What is it?" she asked, with less snark than previously.

"That prick the pack hired as our priest is a piece of shit. He took advantage of Madison and got her pregnant."

"What!" Jasmine exclaimed, her mouth falling open.

"Yeah!"

"Repeat that. I don't think I heard you right."

"The bitchface knocked Madison up."

"Madison?" Jasmine slapped her hands down on her desk. "Our friend Madison who wears a virtue ring?"

"Yes, *that* Madison."

"Did he . . . do it by force?"

"No, but it doesn't make him any less of a dickwad."

"I know, but I just want to understand exactly what happened." Jasmine let out a sigh and shook her head.

"He needs to be fired." Jasmine began to open her mouth, but I kept going. "I want to get proof before we take it to Blake. I know he can just use his alpha aura on him, and Colvin won't be able to lie. But you know how the pack is. They're going to judge her and spread rumors about her. If we at least get a video of him admitting to what a douchebag he is, then at least we'll have that in case anyone says anything."

"Is Madison okay?" Jasmine asked. "Goddess, she must be devastated."

"Well, she's definitely been better," I replied. "We need to end this asshole."

"Did you have a plan?"

"Hell yeah!" I replied, and I think I smiled just as evilly as Blake at that moment, finally understanding what it truly felt like to have bloodlust.

Chapter 16

"Okay, Madison, you know what to say, right?" I asked.

She nodded.

"Don't worry, it's going to be okay." Jasmine wrapped her arms around her. "Even if it doesn't work, Blake's going to take care of the situation. And the pack has your back. We'll make sure you and your pup will have what you need."

Madison stared down at the ground. "I told my parents today. And they were so disappointed in me. My mom basically locked herself in the bedroom. She told me she had to lie down and hasn't spoken to me since. And my dad just looked so hurt and upset. He just went outside to work in the yard. What am I going to do?" A tear slid down her cheek.

"You have us," Jasmine said, squeezing her hand. "We're here for you. And from personal experience, they'll eventually get over it. Especially once their grandpup arrives."

She sniffed and then wiped at her eyes. "Okay, I'm ready." She straightened her shoulders, stiffened her arms, and clenched her hands into fists with determination on her face.

"Are you sure?" Jasmine asked.

"Yeah, I can do this," she replied. "I thought about what Lucy said. That I probably wasn't the first and I definitely won't be the last. I'm doing this for all the other victims. He has no right to call himself a priest with the way he acts!"

"That's right!" I put an arm around Madison, giving her a squeeze.

"Okay, I'm going in." Her lips quivered as she forced a smile to her face.

"Good luck," I said, pulling her in for a final hug. Jasmine gave her a gentle pat on the back, and then she exited Jasmine's office. We quietly listened as her footsteps faded while she descended the stairs.

"Okay, here goes nothing," Jasmine said, putting her laptop in a position where we could both see it, a view of Colvin in his office.

Several minutes went by when a knock sounded on the screen, and Colvin straightened up, closing the book he was reading. "Come in." The door slowly opened, and he pushed his chair back forcefully, standing up. "Madison."

She gently shut the door behind her and walked closer to his desk. "Colvin, we need to talk. I can't hide it anymore. I'm going to tell my parents this week."

"Madison, let's talk about this. There's no reason to be rash." He put his hand on her arm, and she winced in reaction. "What's wrong, Maddy?" he asked in a very affectionate voice.

"You know what's wrong," she replied. "I'm pregnant. I need to plan for my pup's and my future."

"It's okay, Maddy. We can take care of this. There's a clinic not too far from the pack. They'll take care of everything, and it'll be like nothing ever happened."

"I'm not getting an abortion, Colvin."

"Of course you are. It's the right thing to do."

"The right thing to do? Does Artemis agree that it's the right thing to do?"

"In this case, yes. I have an important job, a reputation, a family. Think about how many lives you're going to be ruining if you keep it, Maddy. It's better to think of others in cases like this."

"Is that the advice you'd give to someone at temple if they came to you?"

"That's different. Then I have to act in a professional capacity. But this is personal."

"So you don't live the same teachings that you expect everyone else to live?"

"Holy Artemis, Madison!" He clenched his fists and then slowly unclenched them, giving his head a shake.

"It just seems like you're being very hypocritical. You tell everyone else abortion is wrong. But you tell me that it's okay. Why is mine okay and everyone else's isn't?"

"You know why," he replied through gritted teeth.

"Because it affects you, that's why! Because when it's you who's being affected, suddenly it's okay to break the rules. But not okay for anyone else. It's okay for you to sin but not anyone else!" She stood up and spoke with passion, swinging her arms in emphasis.

Colvin stepped around his desk and grabbed Madison's wrists aggressively, halting her arms midswing.

Jasmine and I leaned forward and looked at each other, both our mouths wide open and eyebrows raised.

Madison yelped and then continued, "I'm going to need help with raising the pup."

"You're a selfish whore," he said in a quiet, menacing tone. She flinched. "First you come in here and seduce me. Wearing your short dresses and leaning over my desk, showing me your tits." Madison closed her eyes, turning her head downward. His grip on her wrists seemed to tighten as the veins in his arms became more prominent. "Only a whore would let me fuck her over my desk. The only thing you had on your mind since you took this job was sin and seduction. And you couldn't stop there. No. Now you're out to ruin my life too—a priest's life. Ruin my life, my mate's life, and my pups' lives." He paused and then mockingly said, "And you call yourself a believer of Artemis."

"Why would you say that?" Madison choked out. Tears streamed down her face. "You told me you loved me. You told me I made you the happiest you've been in a long time. How can you talk to me like this now?"

"Because you are destroying my life, Madison!"

"You're destroying mine too! I'm going to have to raise this pup by myself! And my parents will be so disappointed in me!"

"Then just do what I fucking told you to do from the get-go." He let go of her wrists and seemed to soften. Madison rubbed at her arms as he continued, "I'll go with you. I'll drive you, I'll pay for it. I'll help you with your recovery. If you just get rid of it it'll be like nothing ever happened and we can go on with our lives."

"I don't want an abortion!" Madison bellowed. "All pups are blessed by the Moon Goddess, and I won't get rid of mine!"

"Even if the whole pack knows what a slut you are?"

"Even if the whole pack thinks that about me, I'm not ending my pregnancy. Some things are more important than reputation."

For a moment it was silent. Then Colvin glared at Madison and said, "What a shame if something were to happen to it. Say, if someone used their wolf claws to pull it out."

Madison widened her eyes. "You wouldn't!"

"It's your word against mine." He then stepped around her and stood in front of the door. "Don't even bother trying to scream. This room has been soundproofed for privacy."

Madison stepped back and clutched at her stomach. "You'd actually kill our pup?"

"And the best part is no one would ever believe a priest would do something like that. If you say anything, everyone will just think you're a little liar who wants attention." He laughed in a maniacal way.

"You're wrong!"

He laughed some more. "You'll heal quickly. Too quick for a doctor to examine you."

She whimpered, and he pulled the sweater he was wearing off his body.

"If you don't struggle, I'll be gentle. It'll only hurt for a moment or two," he said far too calmly.

"I can't believe how sick you are."

He began to unbuckle his pants, dragging them slowly down his legs. "If you had just listened to me, we wouldn't be here. But the pretty ones never are very smart, are they? Just a few hours of healing, and it'll be like nothing ever happened. I'll even do my best not to get any blood on your clothes."

Madison's hands shook. He was down to just his boxers. She gripped the desk and said, "Look in the upper corner. In your hanging plant. Does something look different?"

He looked up and squinted.

"You're being recorded. And if you touch my pup, Alpha Blake already said it would be a death sentence. He's waiting outside the door right now."

"What the fuck?"

"So is it still my word against yours? Do you still want to violently rip my pup from me? Any last words for your family when they see this video?"

"You bitch!"

Just then the door swung open, hitting Colvin in the back as Blake and Jack forced themselves into the room.

"I mindlinked him," Jasmine said to me.

"Perfect timing," I said as we watched Blake and Jack pull Colvin out of the room. "I hope Colvin likes the accommodations we have in the cells."

Madison turned to the camera, smiled, and put two thumbs up, swiftly exiting the room.

Chapter 17

The next day, I was putting Libby to bed when a knock sounded on the front door.

"Can you check who it is? I'm just about to hop in the shower," Madison yelled out to me.

"Libby, hold this book, and I'll be right back, okay?" I said, hoisting myself up off the floor where I had been sitting with Libby while reading to her.

I padded out into the common area and crept over to the front door. Who the hell was coming to our door at this hour? I glanced through the peephole and a familiar, movie star handsome face stared back at me. I pulled the door open and Luke smiled, showing off all his perfect, white teeth.

"Can I come in?" he asked.

"Uh, okay. I was just putting Libby to bed if you want to help."

"Yeah, I'd like that," he said, stepping past me and pulling a bouquet of red roses out from behind his back. "Here, I got these for you."

"Oh," I said, a bit taken aback. "Thanks." All of Luke's emotions flooded my body—happiness, pride, and affection. I blinked a few times, trying to think back to the last time I'd sensed that Luke felt these exact emotions all at once. It had to have been during the early days when we'd first marked each other. Those emotions eventually faded into the negative ones that had taken their place, driving us apart more and more each day. "Let me go put these in some water."

"I'll be with Libby," Luke said, slipping off his shoes. He then disappeared into her room, directly followed by a scream of "Dada!"

I searched the kitchen for a vase, opening and closing different cabinets. Eventually, I gave up and just cut the stems down using some scissors and shoved them into a couple of glasses. Hey, it worked.

When I entered Libby's room, Luke's back was turned to me as he tucked her into her crib. He turned with his index finger to his mouth. As he came closer to me, he placed his hand on my lower back and led me out of the room, and I shivered as sparks traveled up and down the length of my spine. It was then that I realized they had previously been dulled. Now they were much stronger, as if they were a reflection of one's feelings toward their mate.

"Can we sit?" Luke asked.

"Sure," I replied, and his hand found mine, enclosing itself around my more petite one. "Before we sit, can I get you a drink or something?"

"You know, it would be nice to split a bottle of wine like we used to." He grinned, his eyes glued so intently to mine it made me a bit nervous. I bit my lip and nodded, tearing myself away from him. And suddenly it all flooded back—the old feelings of how wonderful and natural it once was and could be again.

I found a bottle of red on the wine rack. And, of course, I could never remember where I'd put the wine opener. I dug around different drawers until I finally found it sitting on top of the microwave. I swiftly opened the bottle and grabbed two wine glasses, bringing them out into the living room.

When I sat down, I glanced over at the coffee table to find a present sitting atop it.

"What's that?"

Luke ignored my question at first, taking the wine and glasses from me and swiftly pouring us generous amounts. Once he was done, he lifted his glass up to me and said, "Cheers."

I clinked mine against his and then took a sip while he did the same. After a few moments, Luke put his glass down, and I mimicked the movement. He turned toward me and shifted closer, taking my hands in his, the same way he always had before, rubbing his thumbs against my palms.

I can't lie, the feeling was absolutely intoxicating. I breathed in his mate scent, giving in to the sensations of sparks traveling up and down my arms. Pleasure aches flooded my inner thighs as I suddenly couldn't imagine ending the night without Luke between them.

It had been months since he'd undressed me, allowing his lips to linger along every bare piece of skin, since I'd tasted the salty skin of his cock, since I'd heard him groan as he unloaded himself inside me, and since I'd felt his rough pubic hair under my fingertips as I ran my fingers along it afterward while we'd cuddle together. I missed all of it. I missed being intimate and sharing those moments with him.

I ached with desire, my panties soaked, and my fingers tingling with yearning to touch and explore his body again. It had been so long. Would I remember everything or would it feel brand new?

Our emotions were melding together, and I was so close to saying fuck it, and just jumping into his lap, guiding his hand inside the crotch of my panties. Goddess, I could already imagine how good it would feel for him to stroke me there again, as the sparks danced along the most sensitive part of my body.

He'd be eager. He'd want to rip my panties off and give in to his animalistic desires. He'd paw at my breasts with desperation and grab my hips aggressively. He'd bring his tongue to my clit and lap at it until I begged him to fuck me. As disciplined as he was, he'd let go and take everything he hadn't in months.

"Lucy." He moved his rosy lips, and his voice came out gravelly.

I nodded, not speaking.

"I got you a little gift, open it."

I picked up the parcel and unwrapped it carefully, finding a jewelry box inside. I opened it and there was a dainty gold chain with a tiny heart pendant. It was small and understated, but I could tell it hadn't been cheap. I looked upward and locked eyes with him. "Thanks, it's very nice."

"Let me put it on you," he offered. I turned around, and he fumbled with the clasp, his hands brushing against the back of my neck, finally locking it into place. When I turned back to face him, he took my hands again. "Lucy, I'm really proud of you. You've put in so much work to prove yourself as a beta mate. And I'm absolutely amazed by all the changes you've made and the positive impacts you've had on everyone. What you did for Madison was something a true beta mate would do."

"Is that why you got me the gift? Because I already knew all that. You don't have to tell me. And I definitely don't need some sort of gold star sticker as a reward like some little kid."

"No, I just wanted to get you a gift. As a symbol of our relationship being mended."

"I see."

"I miss you. I love you. I think this break was good for us to finally figure out what's important. And, Lucy, you're important to me. I never stopped loving you. I always hoped we'd work things out. So, will you move back to the packhouse as my mate?"

I pulled my hands from his and stared at him. What would happen next time we had problems? Would he just kick me out of the packhouse again? He'd said I wasn't taking my beta mate duties seriously, but he hadn't taken his duties as a mate to me seriously either.

I cleared my throat to tell him exactly how I felt. "While I'm willing to take some of the blame for what went wrong in our relationship, you know I'm not fully at fault, right?"

I stared intently into his eyes and he didn't respond, so I continued. "You never listened or validated my feelings when I was going through my postpartum depression, and you buried yourself in work instead. I felt like I was forced into being the sole caretaker for Libby even though I never agreed to take on that role by myself, especially while I was also working at the café."

He blinked a few times, and it was clear he'd expected me to just run right back into his arms, no questions asked. I could sense that the happy feelings from earlier were now fading to something more negative and sour.

"Luke, I'm not ready to move back in until you prove that you're willing to meet me halfway, put in the effort required to maintain the relationship, and you won't just kick me out the next time we have a disagreement."

Luke hung his head and let out a deep breath. "I promise I'll prove to you that I can be a good mate moving forward."

"Come," I said, getting up and walking toward the door. I opened it for him and didn't have to say anything. He got the hint. I waited until he pulled on his shoes and coat. After he stepped past me into the hallway I stopped him, pulling gently on his arm.

He turned around to face me and I placed the palms of my hands on his cheeks. As his eyes widened, I pulled his face toward me, bringing his lips to mine. I gave him one big kiss and pulled away. His Adam's apple bobbed as he swallowed.

"I believe in you, Luke." Before he could respond, I shut the door. Goddess be damned if I wasn't going to make him work for it this time.

THE END

Author's Note

Thanks for reading *Wolfbrat*!

Want to meet the other characters in the *Wolfbane* series? Visit my Instagram (@celiahartauthor) or website (celia-hart.com) to check out the other books and stay up-to-date on new releases.

If you enjoyed this book, please consider leaving me a review! Honest, authentic reviews and feedback, written by real readers, are invaluable to authors, especially indie ones such as myself. If you have a few moments to spare, I'd really appreciate it, even if it's only a quick sentence to say you enjoyed the book!

About Celia Hart

Celia Hart is a boring accountant by day and a secret paranormal romance writer by night. Like Lucy, she is overly persistent. Unlike Lucy, she finds pleasure in cleaning and organizing. She lives just outside of Boston, MA with her two miniature schnauzers. When she's not writing, her other hobbies include traveling, eating, cooking, and some outdoorsy stuff like hiking and skiing.

Wolfbane Series: Order of Books

Book 1: Wolfbane

Book 2: Wolfblood

Book 3: Wolfborn

Book 3.5: Wolfbrat: A Novella About Lucy

Book 4: Wolfbitten (Coming Soon)